MURDER ON CONTADORA ISLAND

fred berri

Award-winning author...

Award-winning 5 Star author...*fred berri*

Author of:
Cousins' Bad Blood
Ten Cents a Dance
Bullets Before Dawn-Murder in Chinatown
Adventures of Carmelo...
(A children's learning story)
fredberri.com

Reader's Favorite provides professional reviews for authors and has earned the respect of renowned publishers such as Random House, Simon & Schuster and Harper Collins. Reader's Favorite has received the Best Websites for Authors and Honoring Excellence awards from the Association of Independent Authors. Readers' Favorite also tries to help those in need by donating books and income each year to St. Jude Children's Research Hospital.

"Twist, turn and bend the truth. Now it's fiction." © fred berri

"Great books are weighed and measured by their style and matter, and not the trimmings and shading of their grammar."

Mark Twain

Murder on Contadora Island
Copyright © 2020 frederic dalberri
ISBN: 978-1-7347847-5-6 Print
ISBN: 978-1-7347847-6-3 Ebook

Reader Awareness
The story herein is for a mature audience containing adult material that includes coarse language, sexual content, and violence.

Dedication

Lola, Rachel, Chris, Carmelo, Ben.

Many thanks to Lola with her help of developing my characters.

NOTE FROM THE AUTHOR

This story is fictional. Any names, characters, places, or situations are purely coincidental and are a "fougasse.[1]" Any similarity to real persons, living or dead is coincidental and not intended by the author, with the exception of historical events, historical dates, or any actual locations, and facts.

---

[1] Fougasse /fuːˈɡaːs/ is a term used for "fake" or not real. The word originated back in the seventeenth century to describe a fake rock that was filled with explosives during wars. Soldiers would step on these fake rocks, exploding the bomb and causing serious injury or death. So the rock being fake or not real was termed a *fougasse*. This novel is a fougasse.

Acknowledgements

Janet Sierzant, La Maison Publishing, Inc.
For her expertise preparing this book for publication.

Judith Konitzer for her editing expertise.

Prologue

Betsy bolted upright, heart about to burst through her chest. Beads of perspiration formed on her forehead. The nightmares were becoming more frequent. *Why, Calvin, why did you leave me? It's not right. It's not fair. We had plans. We had dreams. We planned to have a baby.*

I need another drink, she decided, throwing off the covers. She headed to the bathroom. Then she made herself another vodka martini.

"God damn it, Calvin! I'm trying to forgive you. I hope I can one day, and I hope that day comes soon.

CHAPTER 1

Elizabetta was born in 1915, in Naples, Italy, and arrived in New York at age five. Her parents, Frederico and Luisa, were bakers. The Roaring Twenties was a decade of economic growth and widespread prosperity for them, driven by the recovery from World War I, its devastations and deferred spending, a boom in construction, and the rapid growth of consumer **goods**. The United States transitioned from a wartime **economy to** a booming peacetime one, providing loans for those who proved themselves worthy through hard work. The U.S. became the **richest country in** the world per capita and society acculturated into consumerism. Historians frequently refer to the 1920s as the "Roaring Twenties and the "Jazz Age." After many years of working for Frederico's cousin, Dino, who sponsored[2] them, Frederico and Luisa opened their own shop on Mulberry Street where Elizabetta learned their trade.

Over the years, Elizabetta grew into a beautiful young woman, a little taller than most European women, making men take notice her. Soft olive skin similar to an Ethiopian god, and golden brown hair that flowed just below her shoulders emphasized her striking hazel eyes inherited from

---

[2] A Sponsor is a person accepting financial responsibility for another person coming into the United States. to live permanently. Often the Sponsor would have employment and housing already in place.

her father. She spoke fluent Italian, and when speaking English, her accent captivated the listener.

Her parents were not practicing Catholics, only attending Sunday mass when the fourteen-hour workday in their shop permitted. Frederico and Luisa forbade their daughter to date, in harmony with their Italian tradition and heritage. However, when she was in high school, Elizabetta told her parents she was going to Mt. Carmel Church for a Novena, a service of special prayers for nine evenings. It thrilled Frederico and Luisa that their daughter developed a Godly devotion since they never could. Sometimes, privately, they questioned if God even existed. Elizabetta never got to the church for the Novenas, but met her girlfriends and the boys who were always there to take whatever the girls would give. The immature men fawned over her beauty and showered her with compliments and gifts. By the time Elizabetta graduated high school, the only one in her family to achieve such a goal, she was no longer a virgin.

After Frederico and Luisa Gianno died of consumption,[3] Elizabetta stopped using her birth name, using Betsy to fit into the American landscape.

She dreamed of owning a fine restaurant where diners appreciated five-star dining with white linen tablecloths. The Maître D' would wear a tuxedo.

Betsy did not want to struggle like her parents, who had sometimes worried if they could pay the rent. Betsy wanted a change from the hard demands put on Frederico and Luisa. She sold the bakery, lifted herself by the bootstraps, and went to work for herself to earn enough money to live in Paris and train at the prominent French culinary school, Le Cordon Bleu. Betsy accomplished the award, Diplôme de Pàtisserie, acknowledging her as an accomplished culinary and pastry chef, top in her class. She was euphoric, on her way with hope of a culinary career and an exciting future. In addition, a casual culinary classmate led to the icing on the cake: she met the man of her dreams. Betsy fell in love with Calvin Dorsett.

Together, as accomplished culinary and pastry chefs, Betsy realized her lifelong dream was coming true alongside the man she loved. *What could be better? We can do this together. Why not? All we need is money to reach what we worked for–our dreams.*

Betsy Gianno became Mrs. Calvin Dorsett on December 21, 1943. They chose the date with care: The Winter Solstice. Its Latin meaning: *the sun stands still.* They always imagined their love made time stand still when they were in each other's arms. Since both were U.S. citizens, they held their ceremony in The *American Church, Paris.*[4]

---

[3] Tuberculosis caused by the bacterium Mycobacterium tuberculosis
[4] See references page.

Life gets in the way
while you're making plans...

CHAPTER 2

They returned to New York to pursue their dream, but the U.S. Army drafted Calvin on June 2, 1944.

Betsy understood the meaning behind the expression: *Life gets in the way when you're making plans.* Their dream faded on the morning of April 1st, 1945, ten months after they shared their last night together before Calvin shipped out.

U.S. troops pushed through the German defensive line heading into Torgau, Germany, following the Elbe River. German snipers ambushed a patrol killing all the American soldiers, one was Corporal Calvin Dorsett. Thirty-six days later, on the morning of May 7, 1945, Germany signed the unconditional surrender of all German forces.

Betsy hated the April Fool's Day pranks; she never appreciated them. One thing she did understand—April 1st wasn't a hoax or prank when the courier delivered the telegram from the Department of the Army that devastated Betsy.

WESTERN UNION

I-28 31 Govt =WUX WASHINGTON DC 16 10328A
MRS ELIZABETTA DORSETT=
R 15 45 AM 9 30
1868 HUDSON ST NEW YORK NY

THE SECRETARY OF WAR DIRECTS ME TO EXPRESS HIS DEEP REGRET THAT YOUR HUSBAND, CORPORAL CALVIN DORSETT, WAS KILLED IN ACTION IN DEFENSE OF HIS COUNTRY ON ONE APRIL IN GERMANY. LETTER FOLLOWS.

ESA THE ADJUTANT GENERAL

The reality of Betsy's loss remained with her every day. She wished the knock on her door had been an April Fool's Day prank.

Betsy could never work up the courage or the desire to visit The Lorraine American Cemetery outside Saint-Avold, Moselle, France, where the United States buried her husband, Corporal Calvin Dorsett, with thousands of other American heroes. She wanted to remember Calvin as he had been during the scant time they'd had together — *alive, vibrant, and handsome.*

Calvin had been a mixture of British and French blood. According to him, his family history pre-dated 1700 and boasted many nobles who sat in the House of Lords. Calvin's father held a position as American Community Liaison Officer to Britain and lived in London until his death. While his parents were visiting the United States, Calvin was born. He attended Canterbury boarding school, where he spent much of his youth. Calvin spoke English and French with a British accent.

Betsy had once been told, "Listening to you both, one would think you met at a multicultural fellowship program."

Calvin had questioned if their children would be *stuffy* since the Dorsett name derived from words meaning kindness and pleasantness.

Betsy rebuked him. "Don't let kindness and pleasant fool you with being stuffy or weak. *Contraire!* You are a nobleman with character, generosity, and courage! Together, we can beat the world."

They had talked about walking their children to school and taking them to the Radio City Music Hall Christmas show, the matinee Broadway shows, to the Central Park Zoo, and eating at their fine dining restaurant touting a five-star rating.

Her remembrances became tearful. She looked at his picture, whispering, "The world beat us, Calvin."

Betsy lived in a pre-war apartment building in the city's heart. Its masterful architectural design built with majestic form and elegance oozed character. Calvin's military benefits and his inheritance of his parent's life insurances helped pay for her living, a living for Betsy that was empty.

She loved New York City and embraced its magic, the diversity of its people, and the culture. Its buzz and variety helped her cope with the meaningless days of her life.

CHAPTER 3

Betsy tired of sliding Blue Plate Specials along the counter at the all-night Crosstown Diner on New York's 48th and 8th Avenues. Each night she served cops, electric power plant employees, doctors, nurses, security guards, stage performers, and whoever rolled or staggered in from the night shift or from a night on the town.

She walked miles every night, serving food to her regulars and knew each one by name. Many of them shared what was going on in their personal life. Everyone had a story, and Betsy learned from the transient hookers. They would move to other cities or get sick and disappear. Her years of waitressing taught her how to listen and, just like the hookers, to give only enough of herself to satisfy. That's how the ladies of the night kept their clients on the hook. They were after the same thing: to get paid well for the services they rendered.

"Betsy, c'mon, join us. Sit; have coffee."

"You know I can't. I've got to pay the rent this month," Betsy replied, knowing her statement brought a larger tip. Currently in her life, she wanted money, peace, and perhaps to fulfill the dream she and Calvin had of owning that five-star restaurant.

Looking around, she could not wait until August when the diner closed for vacation. It proved to be the slowest month in the diner's year. Everyone was getting ready for the new school year that opened the week of Labor Day or collecting on their last dibs of summer vacations before the local parks and swimming pools closed. Gus gave his employees a month's paid vacation. He reasoned: Congress *is only in session one hundred seven days a year so why not give my loyal employees a paid vacation so they don't have to worry?*

During the August hiatus, the owner, Gus Pappas, had the diner thoroughly scrubbed and painted. He replaced broken dishes, reupholstered the seats in the booths and the stools at the eat-in counter, and repaired anything that needed it. Walking into the eatery each September first was like walking into a new diner. This was Gus's way of thanking his customers for giving him and his family a comfortable living.

The shows on Broadway eliminated Matinees during the month except for one on Sunday. Many New Yorkers fled the city to the Catskills, a mountain resort with headline entertainers like Jerry Lewis, Milton Berle, and Bob Hope.

Come Labor Day, wearing white shoes was taboo. Betsy complied with the custom too. There would be no white diner waitress uniform with her white safety shoes that squeaked when she came from behind the counter onto the black and white mosaic tile floor.

CHAPTER 4

Betsy changed clothes before and after her shift before heading home. The laundry service took care of replenishing the staff's garb regularly. Gus wouldn't have it any other way. He wanted everyone fresh, their uniform laundered and crisp. Everyone had to pass a hand inspection before their shift began.

His Crosstown Diner was not only for the regulars, who knew to get there before the last of the Broadway shows let out, but it had become a tourist attraction. Gus was proud of its reputation and the fame he had garnered because of the Broadway actors and visiting movie stars who frequented it.

After the shows let out, people would form a line waiting to get inside which only allowed them to reach the red stanchion rope. The person who controlled the rope was an expert at admitting the would-be diners and granting privilege to celebrities. Dropping the rope for an exception led to indistinct chatter, neck swiveling, and speculation from the patrons waiting to be seated. Gus's Crosstown Diner was not ubiquitous in any manner.

Betsy worked the late-night shift, not only for the ten percent premium pay but also for the big-time tippers. She went to the bank every day and carefully deposited into each of her accounts. Depending on the night's take, many times the scale tipped in favor of her savings account. The banks promoted savings accounts as part of the American way, like a membership to an exclusive club. They made you feel patriotic, but Betsy knew it was just a savings account with a fancy twist. She liked the idea that the money was separate from her expense and day-to-day funds and often repeated what Benjamin Franklin said; "A penny saved is a penny earned." Betsy didn't save any pennies. She came home with dollars.

Before calling it a night, which was sunrise to her, Betsy would down a martini or two to help her relax. Sometimes it took three drinks not to imagine Calvin's death screams or smell the stench of the soldiers' blood that drenched the trenches.

After the vodka and vermouth did its job, Betsy would touch her lips with her fingertip and press it to the picture of Calvin in his soldiers' uniform. Her goodnight kiss complete, she whispered, "Good night, Calvin. I love you." She followed this ritual each night for the past three years, always thinking; *thirty-six days between Calvin's life and his death. Forgive me God for my feelings toward you. I think my parents may have been right.*

Everybody has a dream...

CHAPTER 5

Throughout the year, Betsy stopped at the Tropical City Travel Agency to collect brochures of what she thought were exotic places.

"Hi Mrs. Dorsett," Dolores greeted her. "I've been waiting for you to come in. Look at this." The travel agent handed Betsy information for a vacation like she was seeking. "This one looks exciting. I believe this is *the* vacation you've been searching for. We may never top this one."

That year, the travel agent's new brochure caught her eye just as she'd selected the agency because its name portrayed a beautiful tropical paradise.

Panama, a country of Central America on an Isthmus. Embracing the Isthmus are islands known for their natural beauty, vibrant music and culture. Panama is celebrated as "the door to the seas and key to the universe." It enjoys a lively mix of cultural influences, one of which is Contadora Island, known as the forgotten pearl and inhabited by the ghosts of Contadora Island.

Spanish conquistadors landed in 1503 with their find of large numbers of pearls. The Spanish originally used Contadora as a customs island, the place where they would count and record the riches they had pillaged from other islands before heading back to Spain. This is where the island gets its name, as Contadora means "bookkeeper" or "counter."

The ghosts of pirates are rumored to roam the island protecting the hidden treasures that were buried there centuries ago.

The hotel on Contadora Island accommodates its guests with great care and individual pampering. Enjoy your dining experience each evening accompanied by live music, dancing, and moonlight.

The evening came without notice. After her nightly routine, Betsy took her martini, hosting three olives, with her to bed along with the various brochures, reading and re-reading all the information. For a reason Betsy couldn't fathom, she went back to the one brochure Dolores handed her.

What is an Isthmus? Is it the door to the seas and the key to the universe as the brochure says it is? Buried treasure, ghosts of Spanish conquistadors, moonlight serenades, dancing. It sounds so romantic. Can I fall in love again--- at thirty-three?

Holding the brochure in her hand like a child holding her Teddy bear, Betsy soon fell into a peaceful slumber.

CHAPTER 6

Finally, the day Betsy had waited for the past few weeks arrived as she collected all her travel plans from the agency. She packed a dinner dress, bought at Macy's on Thirty-Fourth Street, shoes, and tropical outfits that would fit those special nights under the stars and Moon just as the brochure said. Deep down, she knew these clothes were a far cry from the garb she would wear for her upper class, five-star dining restaurant.

"Here you are Mrs. Dorsett; you're all set to go," enthused Dolores, handing Betsy her travel package.

"This is exciting," Betsy smiled, her eyes dancing with excitement. "Please, Dolores, we've been doing business together too long. Call me, Betsy. This might be a vacation you may never top."

"You never know... Betsy. As soon as you're on your way, I'll start my search for next year," Dolores said. "Let's review your itinerary. You will depart from Idlewild Airport on Braniff International Airways. They just opened routes to Panama. Mrs. Dorsett, ah, I mean Betsy, I wish I was going with you," Dolores said, encouraging Betsy's fantasy. "You'll land in Tocumen International Airport in Panama City. From there, you'll take a shuttle to the ferry."

"A ferry?" questioned Betsy. "I don't remember a ferry. I have frightening memories of crossing the Atlantic on a ship

when we came to the United States. I've never been on the New York Ferry."

"Remember? You're going to the enchanting Contadora Island. *The ghosts of Spanish conquistadors, moonlight serenades, dancing.* It's in the brochure… a five-star hotel on the Island. The boat ride shouldn't take but a few minutes," Dolores said with a smile to calm Betsy's fears.

"Oh yes. Forgive me. I remember now," she said, taking it in stride as part of the enchantment, not willing to admit she'd forgotten the ferry ride.

Just a few more days and off I go. Oh! I can't forget to stop in and tell Mrs. Philomena about my trip.

Betsy's concern for her elderly widowed neighbor, Mrs. Philomena, led her to always check to see if she needed anything for herself or the stray cat Mrs. Philomena adopted. Boxy earned his name because he looked like a prizefighter after his eye closed, the result of an alley fight.

CHAPTER 7

The last day of July would be chaos at the Crosstown Diner. It was maddening. All of Betsy's regular customers knew the diner was closing for the month of August and many of them thought the staff would go without pay. None of the staff told them any different, knowing that the tips would be exceptional. It would be like Christmas week when everyone was in a festive mood and most times, a little tipsy from all the Christmas and year-end partying.

"We'll miss you, Betsy. What will we do for an entire month?" quipped the customers.

"Talk to your wife!" Betsy exclaimed, creating a roar of laughter, knowing many of the men didn't care about their wives.

"Where are you going this year?" they asked over and over.

"I'll let you know when and if I come back to work. You never know. I might meet a rich guy, fall in love, or inherit a lot of money." She turned to wink at Gus stationed at the cash register.

Many of the men and some women who frequented the diner complimented Betsy on her looks, suggesting she go into the movies or model for those provocative girly calendars. She took that as meaning, *what the hell are you doing here?* She endorsed the comments, often thinking: *I could. Even at thirty-three, I bet I could, and I'd make a hell of a lot more cabbage than I serve here. Then I could open my dream restaurant.*

At the stroke of midnight every August 1st, Gus flicked the lights on and off, signaling that the diner was closing. It would not stay open throughout the night. The applause was deafening, part of the yearly ritual. Wolf-like howls from the staff thanked everyone for the tips dropping on the table. The customers left, but the staff still had cleaning and the regular chores to finish before they could line up for their month's pay and Gus's good wishes.

Betsy opened the door and stepped outside, taking a deep breath. She whispered as Gus locked up behind her, "Tomorrow I'm off. I will miss you, my city, but I'll return to you once again to behold your magical charm."

CHAPTER 8

The cab ride to Idlewild Airport and the initial conversation with the cabbie began with the everyday polite banter of inconsequential pleasantries until the cabbie asked where Betsy was going.

"I'm so excited. I'm headed to Contadora Island."

"Ah! Never heard of it. It has a pretty name, eh? Somewhere near Bora Bora? Sounds like a mysterious place. You don't mind travelin' alone? You gotta be careful these days. You know, be aware of what's going on around you. Keep your purse close to your side and your money in a different place, if you know what I mean."

"I love to travel, and no need to worry. Been doing it for a few years but I always can't wait to get back to my city. It comes alive at night. It's magical. There's electric in the air," Betsy answered.

"I'll say. Look at all the neon lights. Now that's electric. Can you image what the electric bill is from Consolidated Edison?

Betsy thought, *poor soul. I don't think I'll answer that. He has an exciting job driving who knows who in this magnificent city and he doesn't get it.*

"Do you mind if I ask? Are you one of those models from the Ford Agency? If not, you should be," the Cabbie said.

He didn't give Betsy a chance to answer, just offered his thought as a fact. He pulled to the curb and turned. "Here we are, Ma'am, Idlewild Airport and Braniff International Airlines. That'll be five twenty."

"Here you go," she said, handing him six dollars and fifty cents. Betsy knew the value of service and how hard you had to work for a decent tip.

"Thank you, Ma'am. Very generous of ya! You enjoy yourself; you hear!"

"You're welcome." Betsy stepped out from the back seat while the Red Cap unloaded her luggage.

Not knowing each other's name or where he was off to next is like some poet writing about two ships passing in the night, respecting each other's destination. The signals from the Ship's Bridge to each other were like the pleasant banter between herself and the cabbie.

"Where to Ma'am?" asked the Red Cap.

The porter brought her luggage to the ticket counter to check in before she went to the gift shop. She rummaged through the magazines, thinking reading would keep her mind on other thoughts, like flying over the ocean. One particular magazine, *Femmes d'augourd'hue*, caught her eye. Spending a year in Paris in culinary school and her time with Calvin, had taught Betsy a substantial amount of the French language and culture, so had Calvin. *I want to remember our time together, our year in Paris. This will help. I need that.*

A handsome man in a tailored cream linen three-piece suit, and a cream Panama hat with dark taupe grosgrain band stood next to Betsy by the cashier. His two-tone leather bluchers shoes were tan on the toe and vamps with a darker brown throat and laces. His tie was a shade darker than the rest of the suit. Without thinking, Betsy gave an audible sigh before catching herself. *What a handsome man. He stands out from the crowd in his tailored suit. It has to be tailor made. It fit without a wrinkle. Is he with someone? Is he waiting for someone? He must have a lot of money. I would have liked to have known him way back when.* He approached the cashier where Betsy was paying for her magazines. An unexpected nervousness she could not help came over her, making her fumble. Betsy pivoted into him, looking him square in the eye.

Tipping the corner of his hat, as gentlemen do, he said; "Excuse me. I didn't mean to…"

Betsy hurried to pick up her change and magazines, scurrying off to the airport bar not waiting for him to finish his apology. She sat at a table to wait for her flight. *My God! What happened to me? Why didn't I answer him? Calvin, say something. Was that an accent I heard? Oh Calvin!*

CHAPTER 9

The plane ride was far from Betsy's thoughts which was highly unusual. The magazines and two martinis gave way to memories of Calvin in their small one room, one bath Parisian apartment they had shared. She remembered all the places they made love, not caring it was such a tiny space because their love stood still each time they touched each other in very intimate places. Calvin, Betsy recalled, always took deep breaths kissing her everywhere from head to toe speaking French in his sexy British accent.

Je t'aime plus chaque jour, chaque heure, chaque minute. Vous êtes l'essence du parfum magnifique d'une femme.[5]

Together, with Calvin, as "December 21st" is to the sun, their love stood still. Such memories, never to be swept under the rug, replaced her fear of flying. Betsy closed her eyes and dozed in the warmth and sentiment of her memories.

Without notice, a ruckus awakened her. One passenger, who drank too much before the flight and continued during, insisted the passenger in the window seat next to him move his briefcase from his lap. It kept hitting the complaining passenger's leg. His request ignored, in a drunken stupor, he tried to remove the briefcase himself. Betsy realized the passenger holding the briefcase was the man in the airport

---

[5] I love you more each day, each hour, each minute. You're the essence of a woman's magnificent scent.

gift shop. She sat up to get a better view as passengers around the fracas rang for the stewardess, setting off flashing lights that summoned her.

"Is there a problem here?" she asked.

"None," answered the man in the tailored suit. "He gets unexpected pain in his knee from an old war injury–shrapnel, but he's asleep now. He'll be all right."

"If you need anything, just use the call button."

He caught Betsy's eye, before he answered the stewardess. "Thank you. I will." He scanned the passengers in the adjacent rows, searching for expressions that showed they had witnessed and disapproved of what had taken place. Slowly, he looked for a reaction to him grabbing the drunk by his nape and smashing his face into the offending briefcase.

Betsy realized he was staring at her. She smirked, giving him a quick nod to acknowledge his bravado, only the Captain's announcement interrupted her.

"We are about to land at Aeroporto International Tocumen. Please stay seated."

Betsy's parents told her stories about the Campanian, also known as the Mafia, and their behavior dealing with people in Naples. What had happened was a perfect shadow of that behavior.

CHAPTER 10

Braniff Flight BI70 landed at Tocumen International Airport without incident. Passengers gathered at the baggage claim as luggage spilled onto the conveyor belt.

"Do you require help, Ma'am?" the Red Cap asked Betsy in his deep Spanish accent.

"Yes, thank you. I'm going to Contadora Island."

"Ah! Such beauty. You may find some treasure, Ma'am. Perhaps romance is in your destiny. Just point to your bags when you recognize them. Follow me when we have all of them. I'll take you to our shuttle. It will take you to the Ferry."

There's that damn Ferry again. I hope I don't get sick.

Glancing around the baggage claim area, Betsy did not see the man in the cream color suit and Panama hat. Disappointed, she pointed to her baggage.

She didn't see the drunk either. *He's still on the plane, sleeping it off.* She imagined him waking to find it empty. *Maybe security took Panama hat into custody. I hope...* Betsy's thoughts fixated on him. The Red Cap summoning her to follow him to board the shuttle interrupted her assumptions. She gave a last wistful look to see if the man in the Panama hat was boarding too.

The loud speaker blared. "Last call. All aboard for the shuttle to Contadora Island Ferry."

To Betsy's disappointment, the handsome gentleman was nowhere in sight.

"Have a pleasant vacation, Ma'am," the Red Cap said, tipping his hat as a thank you for her tip. "Be careful now. There's crazy history and island guests still report stories of ghosts. Keep your hotel door locked."

The door to the open-air shuttle bus to the Ferry swished shut. The man she hoped to see on board was not there, so Betsy switched her attention to the Red Cap's warning about the island's mysteries.

I hope I made the right decision, and Dolores is right about this vacation.

A new paradigm...

CHAPTER 11

Betsy awakened the next morning with a warm tropical breeze whispering through the open windows. Each breeze rolled over her as if it were Calvin. Each breeze became a sigh, each a different caress, remembering Calvin's sensual touch.

"Good morning, Mrs. Dorsett. Breakfast will be in thirty minutes."

"Thank you," Betsy grumbled, ambivalent to the loud knock of the concierge who interrupted her aroused state even as he continued down the hallway.

Well, I'll give this all I can. Betsy wiped a tear from her cheek with the pillow. *I deserve some fun and who knows what will become of this vacation. This exotic island has quite a reputation.*

After a quick shower, Betsy was downstairs in the dining area mingling with guests. Everyone exclaimed over the exquisite buffet set before them and the beautiful sunset that exhaustion from her twelve-hour trip had made her miss. Betsy wasn't sure of her feelings. Was she disappointed not seeing the handsome man she now referred to as Panama Man? Or *am I skeptical about island lore of ghosts, treasures and romance?*

Betsy stood out from the other women and she felt uncomfortable. Men stared and struck up conversations with her; they invited her to join them at their table, ignoring their wives. She replied, "No, thank you. Go! Enjoy your wife. That's what you're here for, isn't it?" She imagined Panama Man rescuing her. The married men would scurry away, put into their place by his possessive look. Soon their wives would question their errant husbands: "What did that woman say to you?"

A voice over the speaker commanded their attention. "A bus tour of Contadora Island will leave in thirty minutes. For those guests who are interested, please go to the lobby. The tour bus will be waiting. Please see our concierge for other scheduled activities."

Wanting to get the full zest of her adventure, Betsy abandoned her breakfast to soak up the island flavor and dream of finding pirate's hidden treasure.

The driver helped the women step up into the bus, an old Army supply truck, its top cut off and seats bolted to the floor. Seating didn't matter; it was completely open.

"Here we go, ladies and gentlemen. Stay seated. The roads get a little rough in spots. We have no mountains, but we have hills and rough roads. So hold on."

The bus struggled up the steep hill and came to an abrupt stop. The breathtaking view of the island's clear turquoise water and untouched white sand beaches delighted Betsy.

"If you look southeast, you will notice something sticking out of the water. It is the bow of what was once a ship from the Tierra Firme fleet that sailed from Spain in the 1700s. It is the Nuevo Mundo, meaning *The New World*, now a coral reef. And the beach is Playa Larga… Long Beach. Some guests have found gold coins there."

My God, it's him, Panama Man! Catching sight of a man walking past the shipwreck into the thick brush, Betsy tuned out the tour guide's speech.

"How can we get down to the shipwreck?" She interrupted the tour guide in a loud voice.

"You can get out and explore. Follow that path down to the beach. It's only a half mile to the ship from here and another mile back to the Inn."

Betsy stood. "I want to walk along the beach. Thank you." A few guests followed her.

"Be careful. Its beauty is captivating, but deceptive. Not everyone can see the danger." She heard the bus driver continue his tour dialogue to the remaining passengers.

Betsy hurried along the path, trying not to lose sight of Panama Man. She didn't care who came off the bus or their destination. She knew the direction she wanted to go. Following his footsteps to where she saw him enter a pathway, Betsy felt the scorching sand through the thin soles of her sandals. The sun beat down on her head. She should have realized the sun's intensity, only six hundred miles from the equator, and wished she'd packed a broad-brimmed hat. Following the path about a quarter mile through the cleared brush lined with colorful tropical flowers, each step brought her closer to the rhythm of steel drums, emanating vibrant island music. Suddenly, much to Betsy's surprise, a village consisting of cabanas and deckhouses appeared. A large outdoor open Tiki bar was part of a small quaint hotel. There was Panama Man sitting at a table with another man who didn't look like he lived on the island.

Betsy strolled to a table across from them. She focused on Panama Man, trying not to be too obvious.

"What can I get you?" Betsy flinched; the bartender startled her.

"Martini, rocks," she replied.

"Want me to run a tab, Ma'am?"

"No, Felix. Put it on mine and cancel the martini. Make it two of your special Red Rums," a voice spoke behind Betsy.

Betsy yelped, "Jesus, you scared me." Turning, there he stood, Panama Man. His companion had vanished.

"Forgive me. I didn't mean to. I remember you from the airport and the plane." Removing his hat, he spoke in a mellow baritone with an Italian accent. "Allow me to introduce myself. I'm Basil Caprio." *What a magnificent looking woman.*

"I'm Betsy. Betsy Dorsett. I hope that man on the plane," she stammered, heart racing, trying to calm herself from the jolt of someone sneaking up behind her.

"Oh, that was nothing. He's fine. You know, a little too much," motioning, drinking with his hand. "I hope you don't mind, I ordered for you. Now that you're on beautiful Contadora Island, taste its culture and enjoy its beauty. May I ask? Do I hear an accent?"

Looking him in the eye, she said, "You shouldn't come up behind a woman like that, and yes, similar to yours. I would say you're Italian also?" Betsy questioned.

"I am. Please forgive me. I apologize again. I didn't mean to startle you. I'm from Abruzzi, living in New York, and you?"

"Ah!" Betsy exclaimed! "I'm from Naples. We came to New York when I was five. I have my United States citizenship certificate because my parents became citizens before they died."

"Oh, I'm sorry. You must have been very young when they left you. I hope they didn't suffer. Death is sad, is it not? Death may be the greatest of all human blessings."

Betsy's silence spoke her answer.

"Are you all right?" Basil asked with concern.

"Yes. Uh, a man who quotes Socrates."

"A beautiful woman who is well read."

"Touché," Betsy quipped.

"Betsy Dorsett does not sound Italian." He questioned her authenticity.

"I know. That's my married name. My given name is Elizabetta Gianno."

"Interesting you chose Betsy as a name. I would have said Liza is more fitting. So much more romantic, don't you think? I'm… I'm sorry again, I…"

"It's all right. I chose Betsy to seem more American."

"Come; take your drink, Betsy. I'm staying at the Island hotel. I assume you are too?"

"Yes."

"Good. We'll take a taxi back. It's too hot to walk, don't you agree?"

Basil pointed to the Island taxis waiting.

He didn't even ask about my being married. What is this hidden place? Who is Basil Caprio? We, he, just arrived. How does he know his way around here?

The taxi ride was too quick. Betsy had hoped it would take longer. Basil spoke with such authority and confidence. Traits she admired in a man.

"Here we are. Will I see you at dinner?" Basil asked.

"Why…" Betsy hesitated before answering, "Yes."

"See you around seven thirty? I'll reserve a table."

CHAPTER 12

Betsy was as nervous as a schoolgirl getting ready for her first date. She drummed her fingers, thinking of all she had to do before seven thirty.

I wonder if they have a manicurist here. No, my nails look good. Oh shit, my hair, she thought to herself.

She stared into the mirror, knowing she looked beautiful. It was seven fifteen. Betsy fidgeted. She was ready but didn't want to be early. *I should be late so Basil will question if I'll show.*

Basil jumped to his feet so Betsy would see him as she sashayed into the room. She knew by his reaction that her plan had worked. She glanced at her watch—7:45. Arriving fashionably late worked like a charm. Her saunter oozed attitude. Heads turned to follow her progress.

Basil took Betsy's two hands in his, drawing her close to kiss each cheek, a customary greeting with Europeans. The waiter held her chair.

"Thank you, Basil." She smiled her thanks to the waiter.

"I'm happy you made it."

"Well, I'll let you know," Betsy answered with a coy smile.

"I like that," Basil stated with a direct look.

"Like what?"

"A confident woman, as you are. I can tell that you are sure of yourself. That is attractive in a woman. It adds to her beauty, although you need to add nothing more." Betsy smiled at what she felt was his genuine chivalry.

Small talk led Betsy's narrative to losing Calvin in the war. Life's vicissitudes passed from lips to ears without judgment or commitment just as the wine changed to what Basil called Felix's Red Rum Specials to lessen the tension of a first date.

When dinner subsided, the ten-piece orchestra played, *"It Had To Be You,"* a favorite standard introducing the seductive feminine voice of Savanna Everett.

"Come Betsy, let us dance. You like to dance, don't you? Most women do." Not waiting for her to answer, he took her hand and led her onto the dance floor.

"This song has wisdom, don't you agree?" Basil asked as he drew her into his arms. She felt the strength in his shoulders. His hand fit perfectly on her lower back.

"I'm not sure what it says that's so wise," Betsy answered.

"The song is about lovers. The words suggest the world will always welcome lovers because it had to be. Think of that. "It had to be you." People meet; they fall in love. The world approves and accepts them. Each one felt the other had to be the one. This is prophetic, no?" Basil asked with sincerity.

"Basil, where were you schooled?" Betsy asked, not answering.

"Hmm. I graduated Sapienza University of Rome, and you?"

She pulled away for a moment and curtsied, returning to the slow flowing steps Basil easily maneuvered. "You mean the University of Nobles, Members of Parliament, and —"

"Oh Betsy, there is no need for that. You, too, are educated. I can tell by how you knew Socrates. You speak Italian and English, two languages. There are many ways to get an education, not just at University, as you know."

"Three, actually." Betsy answered.

"Three… three what?" Basil questioned.

"I speak three languages."

"You see. You are highly educated. Probably you own a successful business back in the States. Let me guess. You're an attorney in one of those tall buildings in the city, or a writer traveling for adventure and stories. Maybe a doctor? No! You're a published photographer. I saw you with your camera."

"None of the above," she smiled. "What was your course of study?"

"I'm trained as a psychiatrist. [6]"

"But you don't practice?" She asked, a thrill of suspicion adding to his mystery.

Basil gazed into her eyes, ignoring her question. He whispered, "Liza, you are the most beautiful woman I've held in my arms."

Her hazel eyes did all the talking as she got lost in his *bonne bouche* worthy of the gods. He was an elegant man, about forty, and well mannered.

There's always a morning after…

CHAPTER 13

Betsy slid from beneath the sheets, rolling over into Basil's arms. His presence startled her.

"Good morning, Liza. You are as beautiful when you first appear as when you disappear into your quiescent. I've ordered room service."

Betsy stared into his eyes in disbelief, realizing they were both naked.

Trying to recall the previous evening, clumsy and embarrassed, she blurted, "What the hell is in those Red Rums? And....?" Her brows rose to question him.

"Why, yes, we did. You were exciting. As a matter of fact—"

"Stop! I don't want to hear it right now. Liza needs to shower." *Why did I say Liza? Betsy---Liza---Betsy---Liza. Oh my God! What the hell am I thinking? What was I thinking last night? What am I doing? I don't want to go backwards. I have to keep focused on my dream and Calvin's. But Basil's so captivating. Stop! Calvin, my love, forgive me.* She dragged the bedspread off the bed, wrapped it around her, covering herself.

CHAPTER 14

Stepping from the shower, Betsy toweled her hair. "Calvin–Oh God! I'm sorry, so sorry, Basil. I did not mean to call you…" She hesitated. "We need to talk."

"Good. I like to talk. Yes, we must talk. I understand your anxiety and your Freudian slip of the tongue, addressing me as Calvin."

"Oh, yes. Your education is in the workings of the mind. Tell me what's on my mind, will you?"

"Well, for one, I will tell you what's on my mind—you. As to your mind, you're guilty about our lovemaking last night. You woke, and it wasn't Calvin in your arms. Then you thought he saw us and—his death. What you're not grasping is that Calvin is a hero. He's a war hero who gave the ultimate sacrifice for you and our country. He would want you to be happy, he wouldn't want you to sacrifice your life because he gave his. Last night.… the song we both sang together, *It Had To Be You*", Calvin would recognize his sacrifice was for you to continue living and welcome a new lover that *had to be,* just as the world accepts that life goes on and the lover you met had to be. So, embrace life and all it encompasses. Calvin will never vanish. I will not let that happen to you. I make that a promise."

Betsy's tension eased. Basil's sincerity comforted her. He was strong and confident, not jealous of the love she still felt for Calvin. The world slipped into oblivion, watching him untie her robe. He exposed her beauty, placing his two fingers where she liked him to be.

Betsy recalled her first finger fuck as a teenager, not letting the adolescent boy enter her with his penis. He pulled her pants and underwear down around her ankles, her blouse and bra pushed up to expose her breasts. Their tentative fondling was tacky. This was different; Basil's circular motion aroused her and made her moist. He leaned in to kiss her. Betsy got lost in Basil's hypnotic eyes.

He studied her like he would view a Rembrandt or Monet in the Louvre in Paris. His roaming eyes excited her. Betsy tugged at the sheet, unceremoniously uncovering Basil, an open invitation for him to embrace her beauty. Basil's burning lips met Betsy's and then strayed wherever he found a place they hadn't been. She felt his sure strength. He brought her to the brink of crescendo, pulling back like a symphonic conductor inviting more instruments, controlling the tempo.

Basil felt her quiver, her hands pushing into his defined strong back, helping conduct the rhythm. Once Betsy uttered a deep sigh, Basil knew he brought his musical score to life and to its cadenza.

Betsy's mind darted all over the place. *I don't remember ever feeling like this with anyone, not even Calvin.*

"Liza — I, I..." Basil stumbled.

"Shh!" she whispered, putting her finger to his lips.

Collaboration...

CHAPTER 15

"You are Liza to me, not Betsy. Be proud of your heritage and the sacrifices your parents made for you. America welcomed us then. The world welcomes us now, don't you agree? Although you live in America, you can be a Liza and still fit into the American environment. I am Basil, Basil Caprio, living in New York among a diverse city of many cultures."

"Basil, I gave you more of me than I ever thought I would — my body though we just met. I've only been here a few days. You're so inspiring, so understanding. You make me so comfortable."

"Liza, tell me your life's dream. The time we spoke at dinner, we just touched the surface. What is it you want to do with your life, your beauty, your talent? You didn't tell me what it is you do. I want to know you — listen to you. Please tell me of your time with Calvin."

Betsy opened up to Basil, telling him every detail of her dreams with Calvin. From having two children, a boy and a girl, not leaving out one iota of the five-star restaurant they dreamed of, down to the staff's uniforms.

"Now that you know my inner self and what I want in life, tell me about you and your aspirations. You seem to want and expect more. You seem to know what you want and how to get it."

"We have more in common than you can imagine, Liza. We can spend our time together. I can help you, and you can help me keep the money I've earned. With that money, we can help you get the fine dining restaurant you want."

"What money? I'm all ears, Basil." *This could be what I've been waiting for. Is this fate? Did the ghosts of this exotic island bring him to me? The door to the seas and key to the universe, meeting a wonderful man with money to help me make my dream come true? What else could it be but Fate?*

"Do you remember the man I was speaking with at the Tiki bar?"

"A vague impression. He disappeared quickly."

"Yes, he did. He doesn't like anyone to see him. You mustn't repeat what I'm about to tell you. Do you understand? Promise me, now!"

What am I doing? What do I know about Basil? I can't believe what I'm thinking. Betsy hesitated.

"Yes, I promise," she said.

"This is the situation. After I tell you this, there is no turning away. I need your full commitment, Liza, nothing less. Do you understand?"

"Yes," Betsy answered, looking down.

"No!" Basil snapped, "You must look me in the eye and swear your commitment. I cannot continue without your pledge. You must promise as I vowed I want to share my love with you." His voice became low and intimate. "I'm falling in love with you."

"Oh Basil," she sighed. "I have feelings for you too. I'm, I'm…"

"I know, shh!" Basil leaned in to kiss her.

"I'm ready, Basil, ready to accept and hold in confidence what you will tell me."

"You will accept the consequences no matter what they are? This man is unlike other men you may have encountered in your life—men that you may have known or men that came into your bakery. He is not honorable like your parents or Calvin. He doesn't believe in God, only in himself and his survival. You cannot trust this man. He gets paid very well for what he does."

"Basil, you're scaring me."

"I mean to scare you. I want you to realize how dangerous this may be for you."

"If you can promise me in return that this will give us the life we both want, the life we can have together, and then I will say *yes* to you. Promise me that!" Betsy demanded.

"Yes, Liza. Trust me. This will give us both what we want, together. I never said this about me when we spoke. I want to be open and honest. If it weren't for my parents, I would have been a peasant farmer like them or on the streets of Italy hustling for every morsel. My parents were poor and struggled for every penny, but they loved me. They sent me to live with my mother's brother, a successful wine maker. My father was too proud to take a handout, but he humbled himself for my future. My father and my mother did not want me to be a farmer, always struggling. They sacrificed and my uncle accepted a pittance from my father every month to keep me, although he never needed it, but he had to accept my father's terms. I went to live with my uncle and aunt. They were wonderful. Never having children of their own, they treated me as their own son. I saw my parents every few months when I visited their farm. Everyone knew of their sacrifice for me. I had to be strong and earn their respect for all they did for me. I saw their eyes, their pain, their tears, and their love. Their sacrifices and my uncle and aunt's help put me into Sapienza University of Rome, allowing me to become a psychiatrist."

"That is sad, touching, and an incredible outcome. Your parents, uncle, and aunt must be so proud of you," Betsy said with tears rolling down her cheeks.

Basil realized at that moment; he had caught her in his snare. She was his not only to have and to hold, but to get his money out of Panama.

"But this is where my story turns, where I am today. So, I am on Contadora Island and ask for your promise and commitment as I am committed to have no harm come to me or my family."

"I'm ready, Basil. Tell me."

Basil stroked her face, drawing her to him, kissing her softly, and murmuring, "Remember your promise, my Liza. I had a referral patient come to me, a very wealthy and widely known man. This came about through one of my professors at Sapienza University of Rome via a telegram. The situation came down to life or death for me and my family and Professor Vaccaro and his family, if I refused. You must try to understand the seriousness of this situation. What could I do? Think about that."

"Yes, yes. I understand," Betsy gasped. "I would have done the same. *Famiglia*, go on."

Basil reached into his satchel lying next to the bed and pulled out a folded envelope. He handed it to Betsy.

"I received this telegram two years ago."

Opening the envelope, Betsy pulled out the paper from Professor Vaccaro.

Telegram Arrival from Italy:

Translation:
7 October 1946
Doctor. Basil Caprio
10451 Katherine Place South
New York, N.Y. USA
I am sending you a very important referral living in the U.S.

STOP

You must receive her as your client. It is imperative to each of us and the University.

STOP

Time will reveal its importance and the benefits to our families.

STOP

Professor Carmelo Vaccaro

CHAPTER 16

"Liza, at first I did not understand, but of course I agreed to meet with this influential client. After all, if Professor Carmelo Vaccaro thought it was important, I had to respect his opinion. It was very important—he chose me, Basil, Basil Caprio. Besides, our families might be in jeopardy. The reward would be handsome. Trust is important, don't you agree?" Basil said, not expecting an answer.

"It didn't seem you had a choice, did you?" Betsy asked.

"As it turns out, no! My new client arrived with two bodyguards and her lady consort that waited for her in the outer office during our sessions. I didn't recognize her or know who she was. However, with her entourage and Professor Vaccaro's telegram, she had to be important. My secretary rescheduled appointments and rearranged patients, since her requested sessions ran two and sometimes four hours. It was brutal to see this young woman suffering. Her mother died during childbirth. Her father raised her, growing up in a world people don't know about and most will never know. He lavished her with protection, private schooling, and wealth. She was financially secure, protected, and received a good education—opera and classical music tutoring. She was denied nothing."

"She studied opera to please her father. She really loved a completely different type of music, being an accomplished vocalist and musician who loved the American Song Book.[6]"

"It sounds like a father who cared and loved his daughter," Betsy said.

"Yes, it does, and it doesn't. She became lost in a morass of lies and explanations for many years. Sylvia didn't care about those things. Like any daughter, she wanted the love of her father."

"Yes. I know that first hand. My father gave me unconditional love. I would say her father loved her very much and protected her as well. Why did she need body guards and a personal consort?" Betsy asked?

"This is true as I stated... yes and no. Her father lavished her, as you say, with material wealth. But the wealth cannot give love! As a teenager, she witnessed her father and another man kill two men in their villa in Italy. This is her *real* father, a killer. As her father became who he is today, Sylvia tried to cope with her secret. She has been in a dark place most of her life. She is scared."

"Scared of her father?" Betsy asked before realizing what she was just told—Sylvia's father is a murderer. Why wouldn't she be afraid of him? "From your demeanor, you answered your own question," Basil said. "Yes, he knows she witnessed the murders, not realizing she was there until it was over. Sylvia was supposed to be at school but stayed home with an illness. Her father heard the door creak, turned to see Sylvia. Then she shut the door. Sylvia hoped she wasn't found out. After her education at Sapienza University where

---

[6] The Great American Songbook, also known as "American Standards", is the canon of the most important and influential American popular songs and jazz stnadards from the early 20th century.

her father became familiar with Professor Carmelo Vaccaro, she was sent on a world trip so he could grow his organization from Italy to the entire East Coast of the United States."

"Sylvia's demons would not leave her. She has been haunted for years. She always wondered how many men her father killed or ordered killed. She attempted suicide on one of her opera tours. The doctors could not tell if it was a real attempt or a cry for help. That's why the personal woman consort never leaves her side. Her father reached out to the Professor, requesting the best psychiatrist he ever taught. As it turns out, it was me! Our weekly appointments turned into daily sessions lasting hours. My patients were turned over to colleagues. I saved her from those demons. That is one of the reasons the compensation was so high. This is the reason I deserve what I'm about to tell you."

"I made you a promise, Basil. I will keep it and you will keep yours," Betsy said with conviction.

"Remember, doctor-client privilege, although you're not my patient. You will be the only other person with this knowledge. Not even Professor Vaccaro knows the details."

Betsy sighed. "I'm here with you now and I want to be with you for years to come."

"My patient's name is Sylvia Caserta. Ring a bell?"

"It sounds familiar, but I can't place her."

"How about Paul Caserta, have you heard of him?"

"Of course. Everyone has seen him on the front page. The authorities believe he was behind blowing up the West Side Piers, using two tons of dynamite because the dock workers refused to become unionized. One of our Navy ships was damaged and almost sank. The government tried to pin it on him and deport him, but they couldn't prove it and dropped the case."

"That's right, Liza. It earned him the nickname, 'Two Ton Paulie.' You see how well he's connected to get away with that?" Basil strongly stressed his concern.

"You mean Sylvia is his daughter? Holy shit!" Betsy shrilled astonishment. "My God, you must have been frightened."

"I was, and in many ways I still am. Yes, Sylvia is the daughter of the notorious mobster, Paul Caserta, who runs the largest criminal empire on the entire Eastern Seaboard of the United States, thus the bodyguards. Now you understand the predicament I did not choose to be in, or the threat to my family that constantly loomed over my head."

"So, you got paid well and have the sessions stopped?" Betsy questioned." It's over one year. What's all the hoopla about? I'm not following,"

"Liza, the man you saw me with, informed me that he tracked me here to Contadora Island. Think about that. Nowhere was there any indication of where I was going and how long I would be gone. Not even with my secretary. She knew I would take a lot of time off, and I would check in periodically. These people have ways to uncover information that the government can't."

"How Basil? What people? How do they have that capability, and who was that man? How was he able to find you to tell you this?" Betsy furrowed her eyebrows.

Basil glanced at Betsy. "I have no fucking clue. For all I know, he worked for the government at one time."

"Oh my God! Do you really think that's a possibility? If they are watching you, then they are watching me now. What the hell have I gotten myself into, Basil?"

"Liza, come into my arms. You are not a target. Remember your commitment."

"Yes, but you still haven't told me all of it. I want to know now!" Betsy demanded.

"I will. You're panicking and I haven't told you the entire story. How can I trust your dedication to me and to us?"

"Yes, yes, I know. I'm nervous about being kept in the dark. Not knowing all the details is putting me on edge. You can understand that, can't you?"

"Yes, Liza. I can understand. I'm testing your confidence as you are testing mine, no?"

"Well, I guess I am. Now what? You promised this would turn out okay. Are you reneging?"

"No, of course not. Please change your name to Liza. It might be a good time to do that."

"Are you serious? This is getting—"

"You promised, remember, Liza? Here it is. Tomorrow we go to Panama City. Tomorrow will be soon enough. Come, look at this magnificent sunset." Taking Betsy's hand, he led her to the balcony. "Let us enjoy this time. Each time may never repeat itself," he added, distracting her from the narrative he was spinning.

The early evening was hot and sticky with humidity. The ceiling fan turned slowly to cut the thick air.

"The night breeze feels good, doesn't it?" Basil asked, turning her toward him.

Betsy untied her robe, letting it drop to the floor.

"I will be Liza."

CHAPTER 17

The bright morning sunlight woke Liza. Basil paced.

"Basil, you'll wear out the carpet."

He had to think, not give way to his inner self. *Liza can help me move this money off the island.*

"The ferry isn't running," he announced. "We have to take a puddle jumper to Panama City."

"What? What's a puddle jumper?" Liza was groggy, not at her best early morning. "Why isn't the ferry running?"

"I don't know," his reply was abrupt. "I was told it happens once in a while. A puddle jumper is a small plane, maybe seats six to eight people. We won't need luggage. We'll be back by late afternoon or early evening. I have to go to the desk and book our seats for the 10 A.M. flight. I'll get a table and we'll meet downstairs for breakfast. Oh, Liza, you were magnificent again last night." He walked back to kiss her. *How can she help me get this cash out of the country?*

Liza held Basil tightly. "Why are you so nervous about flying on a puddle jumper? You're making me nervous seeing you this way."

"Don't be," he said, searching to satisfy her questions. "I'm claustrophobic and the plane is small. This has nothing to do with us. This is…"

"I know, Basil," she whispered. "I'm nervous seeing you so upset about why and where we are going."

"No need to worry, my Liza, you get ready; We'll meet downstairs for breakfast." He pecked her cheek and hurried out the door.

Getting out of bed, she stubbed her toe on Basil's satchel. She cursed at the offending bag, and righted it, revealing a gun inside. She grabbed her chest and cried, "Oh, my God!" Without hesitating, she pushed everything back into the small leather satchel—but not the gun. With her thumb and forefinger, she gingerly picked it up and laid it on the bureau.

CHAPTER 18

Liza placed the gun under a napkin and slid it to Basil.

"I just want coffee." She had wanted Basil to order for her. Her glare and a silence so thick you could slice it with a dagger enveloped them, a dagger she considered using on him. Containing herself no longer, she asked. "Who was that man talking to the waiter and pointing to you? He left as soon as he saw me."

Ignoring her question, Basil answered; "Thank you. I thought of bringing this with us today. You know, just in case."

"Just in case? Just in case of what?" Her voice rose. "Now for sure I'm nervous—your gun, people looking for you, maybe to kill you from what you told me, if you don't return the money," Liza expressed her deep concern.

"And yet, you brought my gun," he murmured. "Simmer down."

Liza felt exhilarated, a nervous excitement like the first time she had actual sex at seventeen. Her parents cautioned her, and the nuns in Catholic school taught that sex before marriage was a sin. Their admonitions didn't matter the moment she was ready. *If this is a part of life and makes me feel so much pleasure, better than getting fingered, how can letting my boyfriend bury his penis in me be bad?* Liza felt that same nervous excitement come over her.

"Liza, you looked flushed. Are you ill?" Basil asked.

"I know you're concerned, but how can you know what I'm feeling? The confusion, anticipation, not knowing what I'm getting into? I really don't know you, Basil. It's only days and look what I've given you."

Reaching for her hands, Basil felt her tension. He met her eyes. "My dear Liza, I'm falling in love. Your beauty, your innocence, your honesty, and your cupidity tempt me."

"I acknowledge my strong desire to achieve my life dream. You may call it greed. And yes, I'm filled with those same feelings you expressed, but I don't know if I'm ready."

"I understand. Death robbed you of Calvin's love, your dreams of having your restaurant, the children you wanted together. Many of us have had our plans stolen. Humanity is the thief who takes from us. It doesn't care where we are or who we are when it robs us. Poverty took my parents from me and I from them. We should have been together. We've all had something snatched away. It's like the magician's sleight of hand. And it robs all of us of time. But now, this is our time, yours and mine. We won't let anything stand in the way of what we deserve, will we?"

"No, Basil. We won't let anything get in our way. We will not sacrifice or be victims any more. I want to put me and you first."

"Together, we will conquer what humanity took from us, Liza. Let's go, now."

CHAPTER 19

The puddle jumper landed on the mainland of Panama. Basil hailed a taxi that took them to Banco Nacional de Panama.

"You don't look as anxious," Liza assured him.

"We're off the coffin ride," he answered. He didn't tell her the actual reason he had paced.

Gathering themselves together, Señor Montebello, the bank manager, greeted them with exuberance as he would welcome a friend. "Ah! Señor Caprio, come… come into my office. It is so nice to see you. And who might this beautiful woman be?" he asked, giving Liza a slow once over.

"Señor Montebello, this is my wife, Liza. I want to add Mrs. Caprio to my accounts, and I need to get into my safe deposit box," Basil answered. He chanced a glance at Liza to see her reaction to the name she herself was being introduced to.

"How do you do, Señor Montebello," she responded, and extended her hand. Not skipping a beat, she turned to Basil with a smile.

"I'll need some identification. You understand, Señor Caprio. It's a formality."

"Of course," Basil responded, reaching in his pocket for a passport. He handed it to the manager.

"Everything seems in order. Just some signatures, Señora, here and here," pointing. Basil knew Montebello stared. Liza's thin summer dress gaped as she leaned forward to sign the papers, exposing her well-rounded bare breasts to Montebello's eyes. Basil said nothing to bring attention to the fraud he was perpetrating.

"Welcome to Panama City National Bank, Señora Caprio. Your key for your box?" Montebello questioned Basil. "As you know, I will need that."

Once inside the private room, Basil opened the box, uncovering stacks of money.

"Oh my God! How much is here?" Liza exclaimed with glee. "I've never seen so much fucking money."

"Shh," Basil hissed, putting his finger to her lips.

"How did you do that? How did you get a passport with my picture under the name of Liza Caprio? Is this the money Sylvia Caserta owes you? My God, Basil, this is a fortune. How much is here?"

"This is not all of it," he said, handing her a bankbook from the box.

Opening it, her eyes widened to see the amount posted– $100,000.

"That's there in case I… we have to leave what's in the account and take the cash in the box — one million. You are now on all the accounts, as I told you." Throwing her arms around Basil in amazement, she asked," Is this yours, your money, all of it?"

Basil just smirked.

Upon leaving, Señor Montebello chased after Basil and Liza. "Anything I can do for you, Señor Caprio, and you, Señora, anything, please let me know."

Basil reached in his pocket, handing Montebello a hundred-dollar bill before he answered, "Yes, we know."

"Oh, Señor Caprio, Señora, you are so generous. I thank you a million times. God bless you both," diminishing himself with bow after bow as they left.

"Why did you give him American money?"

"Because he would rather accept U.S. currency. The dollar is worth more than their own. It's been that way for a long time in Panama. You can't believe what that will buy us. If he hears any news regarding our money, he will contact me immediately."

"What do you mean… any news regarding our money? It is yours, ours, right?" Liza looked over her shoulder, then asked. "Is that why Señor Montebello thanked you a million times? To remind you he knows you or we have one million dollars in the bank vault?"

"Hmm, I didn't catch that. It couldn't be. The bank manager should not know what's in the box, only the bank account. Yes, yes, my Liza. It is ours. But there are complications concerning it all. It *is* our money. Do not worry."

"Do you think he knows what's in the box?" Liza frowned. "Why don't we take it and go to New York where we can change our lives like we spoke? I have a beautiful apartment."

"Patience. All in due time, all in due time. No, he doesn't know how much is in the box. Remember, it needs two keys to open, one is ours and one, the banks'." Her obvious naiveté amused Basil.

CHAPTER 20

The phone jolted Liza from her nap after their busy day traveling, shopping, and counting the money in Panama City.

"Hello," Liza answered, not awake. Silence greeted her. She spoke again, "Hello, who is this?" More silence. "I'm hanging up."

"Don't!" she heard. "Is Mr. Caprio with you?" asked the unfamiliar voice.

"Who?"

"You're well aware of Mr. Caprio. Is Basil with you?"

"No," she lied, hearing Basil in the shower. *I'm not answering* this *strange voice.*

"Listen to me, Mrs. Dorsett, and listen carefully."

"Who is this?" she demanded. "How do you know my name? Is this the front desk manager?"

"Mrs. Dorsett…"

Basil entered the room, a towel tucked around his hips.

"Oh, that's okay. Thank you, no room service. We'll be there for dinner."

"Very good, Mrs. Dorsett. Basil must have come into the room. You're a quick study. We'll talk again."

Liza continued the conversation although the line went dead. "Thank you for calling. We'll choose a table when we arrive," she said.

"Who was that?" Basil asked.

"Management suggesting room service."

"Maybe that's not such a terrible idea. We've had an exhausting day looking at our money," Basil said with a chuckle. "Hmm, why would room service call to ask us if we want service? We only had it once or twice. That's strange. I will call the front desk," Basil said with annoyance.

Liza distracted him, knowing well the person who called was not room service. "I'd like to celebrate: go to the dining room, have dinner, a little wine, and dance."

"Okay, but what are we celebrating?" Basil was uncertain.

"Our one million dollars—you know, for our future together. Now, let's have a pre-celebration," pulling Basil toward her. She kissed him, working her way down his chest, dropping the towel to stroke and enfold what awaited her. *This is meant to be. My lifetime dream is not a fantasy any longer... money and love.*

Basil slid his hands to position her the way she wanted. Liza knew what the boys from school and the men she'd been with liked and she used it to her advantage. Maneuvering, she pushed him down on the bed and straddled him. Her warmth felt good to him.

"I didn't wear a bra today," she whispered. "You saw Señor Montebello staring at my breasts as I signed the papers? He kept wetting his lips."

Basil had never experienced a woman as beautiful or as sensuous before. Liza's soft moan suggested to him she had not experienced such satisfaction before either. It was beyond simple sexual pleasure. They had found something new, something they shared. Neither wanted to lose this something, ever! And there it was—the finale.

CHAPTER 21

The usual crowd populated the open-air hotel dining room. Guests came to enjoy the soft evening tropical breezes, romantic orchestral music, exquisite food, and fine wine. The musical ensemble set the mood from the first piano note. His listeners felt each key stroke just by the piano players' demeanor—eyes closed; head tilted. They absorbed the melodic sounds of each instrument joining him—the base strings; slow, soulful wail of the saxophone; the pulses and rhythmic accents of the drum brushes—drawing their audience into an indigo mood. Liza imagined this ambiance in her restaurant.

Basil avoided Liza's unfounded concerns during dinner. He kept the conversation light, not wanting the neighboring tables to eavesdrop on their discussion. The diners at a nearby table distracted and made Liza uneasy. A man and an attractive woman stared and appeared interested in them. When Liza turned to make eye contact, the man pivoted so she wouldn't see his face. She wasn't certain if it was the same man Basil was with at the Tiki bar. *Maybe, maybe not.* This unsettled her throughout dinner.

Once the dinner hour was over, guests placed their drink orders. The easy listening dinner music ensemble traded places with the orchestra. The instrument sound checks sounded like gibberish until the instrumentalists were satisfied they would create a pure sound. Then a riff resonated from the stage, the introduction for Savannah Everett, the seductive vamp singer. When the curtain rose, she appeared in her signature position, sitting atop the piano. Savanah radiated charisma and beauty, charming the audience, both men and women. She wore a red dress adorned with sprinkles of glitter with red satin stilettos, and a long, white stole draped around her neck. Her appearance complimented her sultry voice. Savannah oozed sex appeal. Deafening applause preceded her first note of *The One I Love Belongs to Somebody Else."*

Savannah mesmerized the audience, capturing each note and word with clarity and perfection. She made you feel that she was singing to you and you alone. Her performance ended as usual, with a standing ovation and no encore.

Once again, the ensemble took center stage for everyone's dancing pleasure. Basil led Liza to the floor.

"Basil," she whispered, "you do so well on your feet.".

"Thank you, my Liza. I took some lessons. You have easy moves yourself. You take my lead very well, here and—in bed. I hope that doesn't embarrass you. It's a compliment, you know." He hoped to reinforce her confidence, to expand her short sightedness in the bigger picture of his scheme, and he wanted to soothe her ruffled feathers from their discussion. Liza couldn't stop noticing the man who had stared earlier. He looked familiar, but she couldn't place him as he danced toward them. She clumsily bumped into him, losing her balance and breaking her heel.

"Oh, I'm so sorry, ma'am. That was awkward; let me help you. I'll buy you a new pair of shoes. God, I'm sorry," not realizing Liza did it to hear his voice.

"Are you all right?" Basil questioned, glaring at the clumsy oaf.

"I'm sorry, Mister...," and they stared at each other just as two gunslingers would make ready for a shootout. "I have two left feet as you saw."

"I'm fine. No harm done," Liza replied, picking up her shoe with the broken heel.

"Are you sure?" Basil asked again for reassurance.

Liza saw Basil's pupils constrict, showing his defiance and dislike at what just happened.

"Yes, I'll take off my other shoe so we can dance."

Her suspicion became reality. *I knew it!* He was the voice on the phone with an important message he wanted to share. *But where did I see him?* The evening faded to night, as gently as the sunsets in the west on Contadora Island—but not so with Liza's thoughts.

Clandestine business...

CHAPTER 22

"Basil, why don't you move in with me since we're together?"

"I don't want any suspicions to point to us," Basil said.

Seeing Liza's pout, Basil hastened to reassure her. "You know that might be an excellent idea. They might think I've checked out and they will have to look for me. Maybe... yes, I think I will do that. Liza, you are thinking ahead. I like that."

"I still don't like they you speak about. Who the hell are *they*? *They, they* always *they*."

"I told you. They are Paul Caserta's people, who will try to *persuade* me to return the money he feels belongs to Sylvia."

"Is it all the money-one million in cash and the bank account of one hundred thousand dollars?" Liza asked to be sure she understood.

Basil chuckled at her naivete. "They're not stupid. Her father has accountants who audit every penny. I wish I could return the hundred thousand and explain they are mistaken, that there is no million dollars. He knows it's missing from Sylvia's accounts and it all points to me—no one else in his organization. Believe me, she has plenty more. We'll be fine, Liza."

"Why do you want me to be Liza?" she whines.

"It's on your passport. It's part of your culture, Elizabetta. Get used to it. It's your saving grace."

"Basil, you're scaring me again."

"Stop! Think this through. You're an intelligent woman. We must change our names to agree with what is on the passports. Maybe live in Italy. We may have to change our names again, and who knows how many more times. You can open your dream restaurant anywhere in the world. You committed yourself one hundred percent. There's no going back. You're in it now. Get used to it," he snapped, almost a command.

Shaken by Basil's harsh words, she flashed to New York-- - *my job, my friends, Mrs. Philomena, and Boxy, but* she could not think beyond the one million dollars and her obsession.

CHAPTER 23

The ringing phone startled Liza, like the loud familiar blare of a New York City fire truck scrambling to clear a pathway through traffic. Liza hurried to pick it up as thoughts flooded her head. *Is it Basil at the front desk taking her up on her suggestion to check out of his room? Would this lead Two Ton Paulie's man to conclude that Basil fled the Island?*

"Ah, Mrs. Dorsett, or shall I call you Elizabetta? I see that Basil is checking out. Is it with you, or is he abandoning you? We have time to chat. Would you like to do that now?"

"No! I don't know who you are, but I know it was you who ran into me on the dance floor. What is it you want from me and from Basil?"

The smooth voice continued. "Oh? So, you recognized me? Strike one, Mrs. Dorsett. I know Elizabetta Gianno and what you did. It doesn't matter how long ago; that never goes away, does it?"

His answer almost paralyzed Liza with fear before she realized what he was saying…

"I want you to help us position Basil so we may…"

"I'm back, Liza," Basil said, struggling to carry his luggage through the door.

"I hear Basil. We'll talk again, Mrs. Dorsett."

Hearing a click, she hung up quickly so Basil wouldn't know she was on the phone.

"Let me help you. Did anyone see you come to my room?"

"No. I picked up my bags and came straight here. The desk clerk rang for the bellboy, but I didn't wait. I think we're good," Basil assured her with confidence.

However, she was not so sure. *Should I tell Basil I've gotten these calls… that the caller is the same man who bumped into me while we were dancing? Should I tell him about his ominous tone, about recognizing him? Shit!*

"Basil, now that we've come this far and we're here together, what's the plan? I haven't heard you speak of one. Do you have a plan?" Liza asked, plucking imaginary lint from her pants, chancing a glance at his reaction. "You showed me money you say is yours. You put me on the account as Liza Caprio.

"I told you. We have to think smart. I don't want to always be looking over my… our shoulders, thinking this man or that person is the one to collect the money Caserta thinks is his. I want us to settle down together, to see you happy with your dream. I want us to spend our lifetime together. I know this sounds premature to say, but it's what I feel. I'm hoping you feel the same. It may take a few moves, but trust me, Liza, we will get there. We will get there together," Basil assured her.

"Let's go to the rum bar tonight. It will get our mind off of things."

"The Island people and Island guests who know its location are always fun," Basil agreed. "They know how to party."

"That's where that man was that you talked to, the one who instantly disappeared," *Is the Tiki Bar man and the man on the dance floor and the phone calls the same man?* She tried to remember, needed to see his face again.

"He will not be there, Liza."

"Then there's no reason not to go, is there? I'll wear what I wore—never mind. I need to change. I'll be a minute. Why don't you get us a cab?"

Holding the taxi door open, Basil didn't give any thought to what Liza said she would wear until her sexy walk made her even more desirable. Gazing at her, he let out a deep sigh. Basil realized why Señor Montebello salivated. *She is every man's desire.*

CHAPTER 24

The indoor Rum Bar Lounge filled with pleasure seekers. This was a different crowd compared to the outdoor Tiki Bar. Some stood, and some sat, but all waited for a table. Neatly dressed in suits and dresses, all were drinking. Although the evening was just beginning, you noticed who was with whom and who was trying to be with someone before the night ended. The eight-piece band played on stage, far enough from the ample dance floor to yield room to the sizeable crowd. The vibrant music lifted spirits and encouraged movement. Soon arms and hips swayed to a rhythmic combination of reggae, calypso, bolero, and jazz.

"Ah! Señor Basil and the beautiful woman you left with the other day. Two Red Rums?" Felix asked, not waiting for an answer. "We were not introduced. I am Felix, your host for the evening. The night brings me into the lounge. Anything you would like, just let me know. Such a beautiful woman as yourself must enjoy the dance floor. Trust me; you will thank me for both."

"Thank you, Felix, this is Liza."

"Pleasure to meet you, Liza. I'll have those drinks for you in a moment."

"Thank you. For both? Both what?" Liza asked Felix.

"For the Red Rums and for Rachel Kazz, their lady vocalist who will perform tonight. She will mesmerize you. Such a way about her! You'll see. Her voice is pure as the driven snow and matches her heart. She is magnificent, far above Savanah, your dinner entertainment. Savanah tried to copy Rachel using the same song. You will want to dance every dance with Basil as she weaves her soulful trance. It is a trance, you know. She has that '*sass*'. You know that song, 'It Had To Be You,' by Miss Billie Holiday, 'don't you?" Felix asked.

"I do, but how do you know that song by her?"

"Liza, Contadora is an island, yes, but we still are part of the world. That song is now a standard. Miss Billie is a favorite of mine; we know her as Sassy. If you think Miss Billie is… well, just wait. You'll see. Rachel will give you a knockout punch with her voice and delivery. My opinion— Rachel is the *Divine one, fierce, bold, and sassy-* a top jazz performer. She deserves the big time. There are record producers here from New York, Chicago, and California to woo her into signing a contract.

"Word got out she would be here all month, so they are wining and dining her to sign. She has offers to choose from. I'll miss her. They've already given her write ups... 'Rachel Kazz has all the razz with all the jazz. A star is born!' If I'm wrong, the entire evening is on me. Come. I'll get a table set for you. I will continue to be your host. She should come on soon. Follow me."

Rachel's first note was just as Felix described — *divine*. Liza could not fault Felix or renege on his offer. Basil would have to pay the tab and give Felix a handsome tip. Good service comes with a price. True to form, Felix was spot on. Rachel Kazz had the *jazz* and *the razz-ma-tazz* that embraced and embodied every note and riff in her arrangements.

During one of the set breaks, Rachel made her way through the crowd greeting and signing autographs until she reached Basil and Liza's table.

"Good to see you, Baby," she greeted Basil with a warm embrace and the European kiss on each cheek. When the moment seemed awkward, Rachel broke away to extend her hand to Liza; "I'm Rachel."

"Rachel, this is Liza," Basil said.

"A pleasure to meet you," she said.

"You are not only beautiful, but your voice is — "

"Thank you, Liza," not letting her finish. "You are beautiful. I see why Basil has you on his arm. You may be wondering why we know each other. Basil is a wonderful therapist. He is one of the tops in his field... in the world. Hang on to him, honey. Basil helped me through some tough situations and I will be eternally grateful."

Liza eyed Rachel with suspicion.... *Baby?*

Rachel caught Liza's slight questioning scowl and head turn toward Basil. "Oh, don't worry, honey. Our relationship was professional and platonic."

Liza sighed with relief even though she could not have changed the past but hoped she controlled the future and one million dollars.

"I understand you're signing a recording contract. Congratulations! That must be exciting. A whole different world for you," Liza gushed, trying to keep Rachel engaged in conversation, listening for any innuendos.

"Yes, it is exciting," Rachel, agreed. "Many things in life are exciting, don't you think so?"

"Oh yes. My name…"

Basil interrupted. "Her name is Liza Gianno, and she is from Nobles. Her parents are from Naples, Italy.

"Interesting," stated Rachel. "My mother was from Sicily and my father from Naples. Maybe we are related. What do you think, Basil?" She stretched her arms toward him, palms up, with a quizzical look.

"There are stranger things that happen," Basil replied with a chuckle.

"You must wonder about my name, Liza. Rachel Kazz is not Italian. It is my stage name. I've got to get back to do another set. Will you both hang around? Maybe after the show we can have some drinks. It'll be fun, like old times."

"I'd love that—"

Felix interrupted. "Another round of Red Rums?" Liza was not so distracted her side glance didn't see Felix place something in Rachel's hand. She closed her eyes, hoping when they reopened that she had imagined what she saw.

"Keep them flowing, Felix," Basil insisted.

"Sure thing, Basil."

"There's my cue to get on stage. I look forward to getting to know you, Liza. We'll grab a bite and drinks here."

Liza followed Rachel's sway to the stage, stopping several times to acknowledge a fan.

"Basil, Rachel impressed me. She is everything and more than Felix said. I'd like for her to join us later." *Is she what brought you here?*

"She will be here all month, then on to New York. It took a lot of therapy for her to be in a fit place. I'm glad you like her."

The night could not have enchanted Liza more. Her thoughts were scrambling like morning eggs. The moon was full. Basil was sauve and handsome, like a sensual Italian actor crafted by Hollywood. *I'm in another country, friends with Rachel Kazz, soon to be a national singing sensation headlining at the Copacabana in New York or the Flamingo Hotel in Las Vegas.* As the Red Rums began numbing the past, Liza's thoughts continued. *I have an old familiar conviction, once shared with Calvin, that life is beginning over, much, too much, to my liking.*

The Red Rums draped a veil over her eyes and fogged her thinking. Each dance in Basil's arms made her feel more secure as she thought of their successful future. She gave no regard to a foregone failure.

The resounding applause startled Liza. Rachel finished her show for the evening. She followed Rachel's every step, watched her make her way to their table with blurred vision. She tried to see and hear what was going on between Basil and Rachel, but was having a tough time of it. Felix's Red Rums and the salty, heavy, humid night air seemed to seep inside her head. All contributed an equal share to her tipsiness, but not enough for her not to question the exchange between Rachel and Basil. Liza's eyes squinted with suspicion and too much Red Rum. *What did Rachel just hand Basil? Was it the same something Felix handed Rachel before she went back on stage? It seemed to be a small piece of paper. Dare I ask?*

"Felix, more Red Rums, all around," Basil signaled with a circular motion of his hand.

"Coming right up, Basil."

"You'll excuse me. I have to…" Basil announced in a whisper, getting up from the table and slipping away.

It took a while for all the autograph hounds to subside, giving Rachel and Liza time to get to know more about each other. "It seems you will need a body guard, Rachel." Liza said.

Felix brought another round of Red Rums.

"I—I—never gave thought to it, Liza. Maybe so, from the look of things. What do you think?" Rachel asked.

"For sure, from what I've seen tonight," Liza said. "Think about the upcoming headlines in *Variety*." Her focus shifted. "Basil's been gone awhile. I hope he's not sick. Maybe I should ask…"

"Basil is a big boy. He's been around the block many times. He's been around the world. You know, Liza, he's stuck on you," Rachel said.

"How do you know that?"

"I know that look very well. I spent many hours in therapy with him."

Basil pulled out a chair, panting and perspiring.

"Are you all right? You look a little peaked."

"I'm great. It's a long wait for the john. The size of this crowd didn't help. I'll be okay. How are you two getting along?"

"We're good, Basil. You may have a winner in Liza," Rachel turned to Liza with a wink and whispered: "We girls have to stick together."

*A smooth sea never made
a skilled sailor...*

CHAPTER 25

Awakened by the loud pounding on their door, Basil stumbled to the door, keeping the safety chain in place. He saw three men in uniforms who had disturbed them. "Can I help you?" he asked.

"I am Police Commandant Zapata. Open the door, please."

"I need a moment. We need to put some clothes on."

"Senior Caprio, we won't wait but two minutes. Do you understand?"

"Yes, yes. Give us a moment." He closed the door on them.

"Two minutes!" shouted the Commandant. "Or my men will break down the door."

"What the hell is happening, Basil," Liza asked in a drowsy, hung-over stupor.

"I don't know. Put on your robe. I have to open the door before they break in."

"What's this all...." Liza asked before the Commandant cut her off by walking in without waiting, two Panama Police Officers on his heels. He stood by the bed, a stout man in his perfectly creased uniform and badge, touting his authority. What distinguished him more than the medals he displayed on his chest above his heart was the patch covering his right eye. He spoke with authority and intimidation.

"There's been a murder. We are investigating and everyone in the hotel of their whereabouts last night... the entire night. Let me see your papers."

"Murder? Who? In the hotel? What are you talking about? What papers?" Liza asked in her muddled, somewhat confused state.

"There was a murder at the Red Rum Village. Your passports?"

Liza looked at Basil—frozen with shark eyes.

Basil knew immediately what she was thinking. *Which passport will he show him? Shit!* "I have them right here," Basil responded, going to his satchel and emptying it on the table. Basil knew it relieved her.

He must have had the genuine passports in there. Still in an unnerved state of mind, she continued to cross her fingers, hoping he didn't put his gun back in there.

She watched to see what fell out onto the table besides the passports. No gun, but a small folded paper.

"Hmm. Let me see. Basil Caprio, a doctor from New York, USA. I see Mr. Caprio, you do a lot of traveling. You have quite a collection of international stamps. Why? What kind of doctor are you?" asked the Commandant.

"I'm a psychiatrist and give lectures in many places, Señior Zapata."

"Commandant Zapata, please," he corrected, proud of his government position and disfigurement. "I see. Are you giving a lecture here, Mr. Caprio?"

"Dr. Caprio, please, Commandant Zapata. I'm vacationing on Contadora Island."

"Forgive me, Doctor," speaking with pinched lips, knowing Basil caught him in his own request to use his formal title.

"You understand, we are visiting all hotel guests. No one leaves tonight. We have a full guest list. No one has checked out, except you, Dr. Caprio. You both have only been here just days. Why did you do that?"

"I wanted Basil, Dr. Caprio, to join me," Liza responded.

"I see your passport here, Mrs. Dorsett. I am correct, it is *Mrs.* Dorsett, is it not?" He raised his eyebrow in inquiry to an officer who nodded.

"It is. I've been a widow for several years. My husband was killed in the war."

"My regrets, Mrs. Dorsett. War is tragic. I know firsthand." He stroked the eye patch. This was his proudest medal. She knew by his arrogance. "I lost my eye in the Coto War. If you do not know our history, it was an armed conflict between Panama and Costa Rica over the Coto, a region in Panama's Chiriquì Province along the Panamanian-Costa Rican border."

"You understand everyone is being interrogated, excuse me, questioned." He gave his officers the signal to start a search. "We also must conduct a search. I trust you don't mind." At which time Liza saw an officer rummaging through her dresser drawers. He held up her panties, fondling, just short of giving them a sniff.

"What the hell are you doing," she screamed, grabbing her panties from the officer's hand, and slamming the drawer. "How dare you?"

I know you'd love to get into those... You're all the same, no matter how old or where you're from.

Distracted by Liza's outcry, no one noticed her pick up the folded paper and stuff it into the pocket of her robe. "My apologies, Mrs. Dorsett. We are almost complete. I see you too are from New York, USA. Also, you have traveled extensively. Italy—France—Canada---a few other countries stamped here. Many of the same countries the doctor has traveled. Do you know each other from New York or Italy?"

"No, Commandant. We met here both of us on vacation. Only a coincidence we are both from New York," Liza answered in a breathy voice.

"We do though, have a lot in common coming from the same area and each have an Italian heritage," Basil chimed in. "If you check the Customs date on the stamps, they will be different."

"Your passport reads, Elizabetta Luisa Dorsett. Why does Dr. Caprio address you as Liza?"

"That's my nick name. It's a diminutive of Elizabetta. Luisa is my deceased mother's name."

"Hmm, interesting. My condolences, Mrs. Dorsett. Please tell me your where-about last evening. Both of you."

Basil went into significant detail about their evening at the Red Rum Lounge with Liza interrupting now and then, and their spending time with Rachel Kazz and Felix so he would know they were there.

"Look at this picture. Do either of you know this man?" He showed the murdered victim with a bullet hole in his forehead. Liza turned away, gagging, "Oh my God!"

"Notice his eyes? One is still open, the other shut. That shows his death was instantaneous. The murderer knew how to kill someone... a professional *hit*. Another aspect of a professional hit-- the gun was left there. We can't trace it. The killer removed the serial number. This is a tactic used by professional killers. They don't want to chance being caught with the gun that can trace them to other killings by the ballistic analysis. We may be a foreign county, but we did not fall off the turnip truck, as you say in America."

"No, I don't recognize him. Do you Liza?" Basil shared the picture.

"No, no, I don't recall ever seeing him," and she pushed it away. "Was he a hotel guest?" Liza asked, knowing full well this was the man that bumped into her on the dance floor, the same man whose voice she recognized on the telephone calls to her room.

Commandant Zapata raised his head toward his two officers, waiting for a gesture signifying approval that everything was in order and they found nothing out of the ordinary.

"You say you met here. Both of you are here such a short time and yet both of your passports were together in the Doctor's satchel and now you share the same room." He turned to Liza; his suspicion defined by his raised eyebrow. "So, Dr. Caprio, being a psychiatrist, you can write prescriptions, dispense narcotics, I assume."

Without giving either a chance to respond, the Commandant continued, "I will check with everyone you said you were with, including the bartender, Felix. Can they vouch for you? Were you in their sight the entire night? I will also track down the singer," snapping his finger, looking up as though trying to remember her name.

"Yes, Commandant, I understand," Basil acknowledged.

"Rachel---Rachel Kazz," Liza said.

"Yes, that is her name. Thank you, Doctor. Thank you both for your cooperation. We shall continue our investigation. The hotel knows that no one can check out without my approval. I hope you understand. Enjoy your stay on Contadora Island. It is beautiful, of course, without such a tragedy. Good day."

"Good day, Commandant," Basil replied as Zapata and his men took their exit.

"What the hell is that about?" Liza exhaled. "I expected him to click his heels."

"We're in a foreign country. They do things differently from what we are used to. And we are foreigners to them even though the United States has a stake here."

"Basil, you know and I do, that was the man who bumped into me on the dance floor. Now I know I recognize him from the Tiki Bar. He was the man you were talking to the day I met you. He was the man staring at us throughout dinner. He called the room a few times."

"What do you mean he called our room a few times?" Basil demanded, anger adding volume to his voice. "Why didn't you tell me? Didn't you think that was important to share?"

"This is happening too fast. I need to sit." Liza answered, holding her head. "I had to be sure, so I created that scene on the dance floor to hear his voice. It was him. I'm sorry I didn't tell you. I recognized his voice from that night. I suspected him when he stared--- that's why I bumped into him.

"What are you talking about? You must tell me everything. We cannot and will not keep anything from each other. We must have complete trust."

"Okay, I will. Sit down."

CHAPTER 26

"Liza, if we are to make a life together, you must be honest and upfront with me. Remember your promise. You said you are in all the way. I don't want to doubt you. This man must have been dangerous. Why else would he have a bullet in his forehead? Whatever he was after could have cost us our lives. I have people looking for me, for the money."

"Basil, I'm sorry. It will never happen again. He wanted to speak with me about you. He wanted to tell me something about you. I was—" She stammered, "I don't know—frightened. It seemed he would expose you. I didn't want any charades. You know---disappointments that unveiled what you might be hiding. How long do we have to look over our shoulder before you can say we're free and the money is ours?"

"Why would I hide anything from you?" he frowned. "I told you I'm falling in love with you. I want to spend my life with you. I thought you felt the same," misdirecting her question, looking hurt.

"Basil... I do. I have feelings of love for you too. I want to be with you even more than I wanted to be with Calvin. This is hard to digest. I feel I've known you a lifetime, and it's only—"

"Okay," he interrupted. "Then we are committed to each other. We are in business together, no?" He smiled as he asked the rhetorical question. Embracing her, he kissed her as she lifted on her tippy toes to return the embrace. She sighed, but he did not know if it was one of relief or a sigh of passion. He kissed her behind her ear, tantalizing Liza's sensitive zone.

Whispering, Liza asked between exhales, "Where are the other passports and your gun? You were gone a long time, Basil. That man in the picture upset you when he bumped into me. Did you…?"

She felt his breath on her skin, answering; "Here, here it is," moving her hand where he wanted to feel his erection. "The other passports are at the bank in the safe deposit box."

"I'm glad you kept your gun on you." *His stamina just keeps going. I never want it to stop.* Her loose robe exposed her breasts, enough to make a suggestive appearance.

They scrambled to the bed where they were sleeping off the effects of the night before just minutes earlier.

CHAPTER 27

Wrestling with her conscience, Liza wanted more dialogue about the night before and Basil's lengthy absence. *I need some answers.* The harsh ring of the telephone interrupted her thoughts. "Hello."

"Mrs. Dorsett, this is Commandant Zapata. I am sending a boat for you and Mr..... excuse me, Dr. Caprio."

"What? Why and where are we going?"

"Liza, who is that? Hand me the phone," Basil demanded, taking control. "Who is this?"

"Ah, Doctor Caprio, this is Commandant Zapata. I explained to Mrs. Dorsett, I am sending a boat for you. You will join me at my Headquarters."

Realizing Basil was distracted, Liza reached into her pocket to read the folded paper that spilled from his satchel. "He is here." *I seem to get sidetracked when I ask about something. He explained that his gun and the fake passports are in the safe deposit box at the bank. How did I miss that? I never left his side...*

"And why is that?" Basil asked the Commandant.

"All in due time, Doctor. I will wait..." Click!

"What's this about Basil?"

"He wants us to join him at his Headquarters. He said he'll explain when we get there."

Liza had a lot of unanswered questions, but she's consumed with the money. *One million dollars! All that lovely money staring me in the face, bundled nice and neat, and stacked with such care.*

A small bus waited on the dock to take the passengers into town. The two single men and the lone woman kept silent. Their eyes looked heavenward—a sign of what they were thinking and what they would say. The three other couples whispered among themselves—their stories and their stories alone might or might not excuse them from any homicidal suspicions.

"Basil, this bus reminds me of a similar one on a trip Calvin and I took while living in France. A youthful man got on holding a chicken. The bus driver told him he couldn't bring a live chicken on the bus. The man twisted the chicken's neck and said," *plus de Poulet vivant.*

"Which means?" Basil asked.

"No more live chicken. I was the only one that gasped. I guess to the others, it was expedient or an everyday occurrence. He knew he would kill the chicken soon, and there were no live chickens allowed on the bus. So why not now? It solved his quandry and the bus driver's at once."

"It was a means to an end for both of them. Interesting, he made it simple with no regrets," Basil observed. "He solved two problems with a swift hand."

There were quite a few hotel guests on the boat being escorted by Panamanian police officers to the Commandant's Headquarters.

"Does anyone know what this is about?" Basil asked of the guests on the boat with them. The Commandant summoned a total of eleven: three couples plus Basil and Liza, two single men, and one woman.

One man answered, "Some bullshit about that murder the other night at the Red Rum Lounge. I don't know why they chose me or any of us."

"This is only the beginning," the other man sitting alone said. "I say they will haul in everyone from the hotel. Look at this piece- of- shit boat. It barely holds us and the crew. They have to take only a few of us at a time."

"Okay, I'll bite," stated the single woman. "Why did they pick us to start?"

"I say it's because our stories have holes in them," another man pitched in. The woman with him, presumably his wife, added, "Why don't they question us at the hotel like they did the other day?"

"It's a tactic they used to get us into unfamiliar territory," stated the independent man. "We'll be in his turf. It's supposed to knock your equilibrium off, so to speak. So, my suggestion is you rehearse your stories. This Commandant is grasping at straws."

"You sound like you have experience in this interrogation," said Liza.

"Never mind about me, sister; worry about yourself. This is serious. Even though the United States controls the Panama Canal Zone and the United States Army is here, we're still in the Republic of Panama, a foreign country — their rules, their way."

The crew escorted them to the Commandant's office.

"Good day. Thank you for coming," Commandant Zapata greeted them.

"Did we have a choice?" asked the single woman Liza recognized from the room next to theirs at the hotel. "I'm on vacation and spent a lot of money to come here. I hoped to meet a man and fall in love, a possibility my travel brochure suggested. Now I'm being investigated because someone murdered a man."

My brochure suggested the same thing. Liza felt a twinge of empathy with the woman.

One by one they escorted them into the Commandant's office.

"Ah, yes, Señora. I understand *your* concern," Zapata addressed the single woman. "We are all concerned in the Republic of Panama when murder is committed."

"I guess you didn't understand me. I came here looking for love, a man. I'm not a Señora. I'm a—"

"Forgive me," he interrupted. "Señora soltera, an unmarried lady. My true wish is that you find love and happiness on Contadora Island. It would be my pleasure to perform the wedding ceremony, if you would grant me the privilege." He heard snickering as she hid her hand in her lap and gave him the finger.

"We will separate you. We will provide each of you with paper and pen to write every minute of the night in question. Then I will speak with you."

"You spoke with us the following day at the hotel," said one of the single men.

"That was a preliminary questioning," Zapata answered. "Quiet! Let's get started." Raising his voice, he ordered in a loud, precise command, "Follow the officers."

"Basil, I'm worried," Liza whispered.

"It's okay. Be honest in what you say. We rehearsed our story. I don't want any conflict. Remember the time line, when I left the table and returned. Trust me, Liza."

"I do, Basil, I do."

"No talking from here on," shouted one of the escort officers. "Follow me."

They ushered each person to a separate room with pen and pad to recap their entire evening at the Red Rum Inn in minute detail.

"Can I go now?" asked the same woman who uttered sarcasm earlier. "I gave you everything you asked for."

"You can wait on the bus to take you back to the boat, if you wish. Or you can wait here and enjoy refreshments while the others finish," answered Commandant Zapata.

She muttered just loud enough for someone to hear, "Fuck you."

It took a while for each person to emerge from their solitary room. Each one drank from the same poison—weakened, reduced, and running on empty.

"Thank you. I will be in touch with you soon. You may board the bus back to the boat. Enjoy your evening," the Commandant said.

Basil grabbed Liza's arm to bring her closer so no one else would hear. "I want to go to the bank. I need to check something."

"No!" exclaimed Liza, her voice harsh. "I want to wear the same thing I wore the day I met Señor Montebello. If we want him to help us, even with your generosity, he must keep thinking he has a chance with me—at least in his dreams."

The bus stopped on the dock. As they exited and walked toward the boat that taxied them to headquarters, another group waited to board the bus that would take them to Commandant Zapata. Basil caught the eye of a man passing. Both nodded once, an acknowledgment.

"Who was that, Basil? Do you know him?" Liza asked. He was silent for a moment.

"Maybe your metaphor of the chicken has more meaning than you think," he smiled, pulling her closer.

Liza didn't understand how it related until much later. She brushed it off as so much psychological babble. "I need a nap before tonight. Let's go back to the room."

"We'll have dinner and drinks. I agree; we'll go to the bank tomorrow."

CHAPTER 28

"Basil, I want to go to the Panama City National Bank today as we agreed."

"All right, is there something in particular you want there?"

"You know fucking well what I want, *Baby*." Her sarcastic reference to Rachel's familiarity went over Basil's head. *"I want to see the gun you said is there. You must have used your magical sleight of hand, and I want to see the fake passports."*

"Whoa! Don't blow a fuse, Liza. Is Commandant Zapata getting to your psyche?"

"You know all about the psyche, don't you, *Baby*, with your left brain—right brain shit!"

"That's correct. I do and you're thinking right brain, which dominates feelings—imagination—intuition. I will show you what your right brain is questioning. Your left brain is processing thoughts such as step-by-step progression where you must bring out a response to a step before taking another step. With you, Liza, they are at war!"

They were silent with their thoughts.

Basil tried to pass his calm to Liza during the brief ride to the Panama City National Bank from the ferry's dock. She seemed edgy.

"Ah, Señor and Señora Caprio. My arms welcome you both," Señor Montebello announced in a voice that echoed in the vast marbled lobby when he saw them enter. He jumped up from his desk and rushed to them.

"I bet he'd love his arms and hands to reach places on me," Liza whispered to Basil.

"Shh! We don't want to upset him."

"I'll take care of him, Basil."

"My warm welcome to you both." He shook Basil's hand and lifted Liza's hand to his lips with an ever so gentle kiss. "The sun rises on the horizon to bring hope of another day. You make such a beautiful couple. I hope to service you anyway I can," Basil noticed Montebello's gaze turn to ogle Liza, hoping for another look down her summer dress at her breasts. Liza knew how to play the game and obliged his bulging eyes by a curtsy low enough for him to get a sneak preview.

"We need access to our box," requested Liza not waiting for Basil.

"Ah! Magnifico. I'll get the key and as *necesario*, I need your key."

"Let us enter the *bõveda*. Oh, pardon, I shall say vault. Choose whatever room you wish. I am at your command. I'm sure you heard by now—such a tragedy on Contadora, wouldn't you say?" he said. "Murder and no less than a United States Marshal. If you need anything, I'll be at my desk." Bowing, he left the vault.

"*Baby*, did you hear what he said? That murdered man was a United States Marshal. The Commandant didn't mention that! Why would a U.S. Marshal be here and wind up getting murdered? Why was he with you at the Tiki Bar?"

Quickly, Basil sidetracked her; "Liza, look! Here is the gun and the passports you so worried about. Are you satisfied?"

How the fuck did he do that? I did not leave his side when we were here. And now, everything is here – the gun, our cash, the passports – the passports with the name Caprio.

Returning the key to Montebello's desk, Liza leaned to give him a better look at her breasts, lingering long enough to imagine his inaudible sigh, knowing she aroused him.

"Here is your key."

"Many thanks, Señora." Montebello responded, licking his lips without realizing he revealed his desires.

"Tell me, how do you know the person murdered on Contadora Island is or was a United States Marshal?" Liza asked without moving, giving Montebello a front-row seat to a show.

Without lifting his eyes, Montebello answered; "Commandant Zapata was in with a signed warrant from the Supreme Court of Justice. There were so many. Some of them were from our police and some from the Department of State's Diplomatic Security Service. He caused a lot of excitement. I had to be there when they opened the box with the key registered to Señor Henry Bradshaw, the U.S. Marshal."

Keeping Montebello mesmerized, Liza continued to question him. "Wow! That had to be scary for you, no?" Drawing into question his manhood.

"Oh no, no Señora," he answered with a slight chuckle. "No, not for me," patting his chest. "I was there. I had to open the box, and we inventoried it."

"That must have seemed like finding treasure, like the pirates left on Contadora Island."

"It contained lots of cash in United States dollars, over one hundred thousand dollars. He must have been working a big international case since they only found his credentials and the key to his box on his person." Montebello came to his senses, realizing his stare had become presumptuous.

"Thank you, Señor Montebello. We must be going. You've been most gracious... Liza?" Basil hinted Liza stop the questioning, that they should leave.

"The pleasure has been all mine. I eagerly await your return," Montebello said, smiling as Basil handed him a hundred-dollar bill.

Liza felt his eyes follow her sashay all the way past the doors, tilting his head to watch as she withdrew from his sight.

"Nice, Liza, quite nice," whispered Basil. "So, what did you get out of that?"

"He was a dirty agent. What was he doing here, and why did he want to talk to me without you around? He knew our names. He knew the different names you used. He had one hundred thousand dollars in his box. The Commandant is playing us, all of us at the hotel. He's holding back, not figuring that we would find out just by letting Montebello get lost in my breasts."

"Let's celebrate at the Red Rum Lounge," Basil suggested.

"What are we celebrating, *Baby*?" Liza questioned.

"My getting lost."

"Huh?"

"Celebrating getting lost in the same way Montebello's eyes got lost."

"You always know the right thing to say. So, tell me where you were when I woke up from my nap the other day; you were not in the room."

"Yes, I know my Liza. I did not want to disturb you. I went for a drink in the bar downstairs, and what's with this Baby you are calling me?"

"Thank you, but I would have liked to go with you. Next time ask me?" Letting him know not to dismiss her. "I thought you liked Baby. Rachel calls you that—*Baby.*"

CHAPTER 29

"Good evening, my friends," the bartender greeted in tune with his untethered eyes He measured Liza without scruples. "How may I be of service?"

Fucking men are all the same. They think with their small head. "The usual," Liza said.

"Ma'am?" questioned the bartender.

"Who are you and where is Felix?" Basil asked with furrowed eyebrows. "He knows our drinks; his famous Red Rums."

"He knows how we *devour* them," Liza quipped, knowing this man would love to devour her as his eyes moved once again from her head to toe and back up again, stopping at her breasts.

"My name is Julio. Felix has not been here the past few days."

"Did something happen to him? Oh, this is Liza, and I'm Basil."

"Happy to be of service. No one knows where Felix is. He's MIA. No one has heard from him."

"What does that mean, MIA?" Liza asked.

"Missing in action," Julio replied. "Are you folks enjoying your stay here on the Island?" He served their Red Rums, trying to make polite conversation.

Ten days. Liza thought with a sense of power. *We met and within ten days we're living in the same hotel room, sharing one million dollars.*

"There's been a lot of excitement since the murder. We've doubled our business. You know, people want to see or hear firsthand someone else's tragedy. We are all being questioned. They found the body close by. They asked me if I saw or heard anything out of the ordinary that night. I said no because I didn't. I was serving the inside lounge with Felix." He gave Basil a direct look to let him know he saw him that night. "It was busy. I assume from what you said, you both were here. Did you see anything strange?" Julio questioned.

"No, How about you, Liza, can you remember anything out of the ordinary?" Basil questioned her without hesitation.

Liza looked at Basil and quirked an eyebrow. *Are you fucking kidding me? You took a powder and left me for more than an hour. That's out of the ordinary.*

"Can't say I did," she said, not missing a beat.

"Rachel is on tonight. It's her last gig until the end of the month, then she moves on to her recording contract and other appearances. I'll be here at this station throughout the evening."

"Oh good, let's see Rachel again after the show," Liza suggested to Basil.

Rachel made her way to Basil and Liza's table after working her way through the crowds. They still kept coming for pictures and autographs after she sat. Some fans wondered who she was with and asked for Basil and Liza's picture and autographs as well, mistaking them for up-and-coming Hollywood stars or record producers. Liza and Basil obliged, thinking it was a hoot.

"As we agreed, Liza, it's these fans that got me where I'm going. I have to do this. You seem to enjoy it. You have Hollywood written all over you. You are more beautiful than Ava Gardner.[7]"

"We have our plans, Rachel. Don't give her any ideas." Basil commented. "You know how hard and how many years you struggled to get here."

"Don't forget my years of therapy during all my growing as a singer."

"How could I? You—"

"Never mind, Basil, we're here now, and so is Liza. You seem to have a future together. I'm jealous. No matter how hard I tried, Liza, Basil kept our sessions on a professional level. That's one reason, I am a success. He taught me to keep my eye on my destination, not waver or get off at every train station to take up with stragglers without a destination, leading nowhere."

Basil threw a casual inquiry into the conversation. "Rachel, Julio mentioned that Felix hasn't been here in a few days."

"Now that you mention it, I haven't seen him. Between all my meetings with the producers and rehearsals, I'm not in tune, if you will, to the outside world at the moment. So, I guess you haven't seen him either?"

"No!" Liza answered. *You were in tune enough to give the note Felix gave you to Basil.* "Rachel, the other evening I saw Felix hand you a piece of paper which you passed to Basil. What was it?"

Basil and Rachel exchanged a startled look. "It was something stupid. Felix gave me his telephone number. I

---

[7] See References

gave it to Basil to return to Felix. I thought Basil could handle Felix. You know, let him down easy. Something I learned in Basil's therapy."

Rachel and Basil felt the boat rock a little. Liza knew what the note said. She saw it the day Zapata came to search their room, and it fell from Basil's satchel. Rachel was lying.

CHAPTER 30

Basil and Liza entered the hotel lobby on their way to morning breakfast. Basil stopped for the morning paper, *La Estrella de Panama,*[8] printed both in Spanish and English for the tourists. This morning's banner headline screamed.

UNITED STATES MARSHAL MURDERED ON CONTADORA ISLAND.
AUTOPSY REVEALS AGENT INGESTED DRUGS BEFORE DEATH.
OVER $100.000 IN CASH U.S. FOUND TIED TO AGENT.

Story page 3 by Ruben Guzman

"Basil, it's all over the newspapers!" Liza exclaimed.

"What do you expect? Murder is front-page news. It doesn't matter what country you're in. Do you think the U.S. has a monopoly on headline news," Basil questioned, not expecting an answer.

"No... no... I mean. I don't know.... Let's go back and order room service."

"Okay, that sounds good. I'll order at the desk. Get the elevator," Basil directed.

---

[8] The Star of Panama

As soon as he put the key in their door, he continued. "Look, hold yourself together. This questioning is far from over. I want to get the money out of the bank and out of Panama so we can take it with us to New York."

How did you get it into the country? We'll get it out the same way. "Basil, why would a US Marshal be talking to you at the Tiki Bar then turn up dead?"

"He told me he was here concerning a matter for Paul Caserta. He came to collect the money I told you about, the money Sylvia paid me from her trust. He didn't work for Sylvia's father but somehow he found out about the money her father wanted returned. He was strong-arming me. If I paid him a portion of the money, he wouldn't tell Two Ton Paulie where I was. He thought we would both benefit if I accepted his deal. I don't know why he turned up dead. He was a dirty cop. We need to keep focused. I think the Commandant will gather everyone for more questioning soon. Remember, he said no one leaves the island without a clearance. He has everyone's passports. No one's giving him the bum's rush."

"Yes, but we have our other passports in the bank box. We were just there and so were they."

"Now you're talkin' and you're on the same page with me. We don't have to be behind the eight ball. This is a new chapter in our lives, Liza. We'll write a great ending as we turn the pages."

"Oh Basil, you know how to calm the waves. I guess that's your psychiatrist training in the ways of the mind."

"It's also because of my affections for you." He kissed her, nibbling her neck, giving her chills. "Here, take this." He reached into his pocket, then held out his hand.

"What is it?"

"Something to calm you down."

The sound of his zipper emphasized the quiet of the room.

She used the expertise that every man hoped for. "Feel my passion," she whispered.

"I do. I love your passion."

They undressed with abandon, throwing their clothes to the floor. Basil joined her on the bed. She felt his erection, causing her body to tighten, and her back to arch as he eased into her. Together they caught the momentum, banging the headboard rhythmically against the wall. Her breath rasped in between her words. "Right there" gasp, "don't stop," gasp! Knowing this would be quick, she sometimes added to her own pleasure, bringing her to a greater climax. They lingered for a moment—Liza wanted to store this in her pleasant memory, not like past ones.

Just before Liza started her usual leisurely gait to the shower, there was a knock on their door.

"Room service."

CHAPTER 31

Frantic knocking on the door became a repetitive occurrence, this time accompanied by shouting. "Everyone down to the dining area—everyone down to the dining area." Basil opened their door to see the cause of the commotion: uniformed police walking up and down the halls, banging and repeating, "Everyone down to the dining area." The sound echoed from floor to floor.

"What the hell is going on?" Basil asked the officer as he passed his door.

Ignoring Basil, he kept walking and knocking. "Five minutes, downstairs, or we will come and get you."

"Jesus Christ, Basil! It's 6 am. Is there a fire? What's happening?" Lisa asked.

"The Commandant's roll call again. He's using a method to affect everyone's psyche and throw everyone off balance with his unexpected visit this early in the morning. See how you questioned what was going on? He's brilliant with his act, trying to seem like a stumblebum. He got to you, your mind and spirit."

Burying her head under the covers, Basil heard her mumble; "Now what?"

"I don't know. Let's get down there."

The dining room filled with guests.

"Everyone here and accounted for, Commandant," saluted an officer.

"Good," Zapata said. "It is with regret that I am getting..." with a deep sigh, he paused. "I am getting a bad feeling... a very bad feeling about what is happening on the island... *my island!* You all know there was a murder. You probably read in today's newspaper the person murdered was a United States Marshal. For those of you who do not know, the Marshal's Service apprehends fugitives from around the world. Agent Henry Bradshaw was an American agent working out of the Dominican Republic. He registered with my office and was tracking a wanted fugitive. All he could tell me is... he was searching for a wanted criminal, a resident of the United States who was reported to be in Panama. Now Agent Bradshaw is dead!"

Zapata walked among the hotel guests, asking in a conversational tone, "Could one of you be that person... the one he was searching for? Most of you are from the United States." His voice rose. "Now, there has been another murder. For you who frequent the Red Rum Inn Lounge and the outdoor Tiki bar, another body has been found." The gasps and murmurs grew.

"Quiet. Please listen. Many of you may have come in contact with the victim. It is... was Felix, the bartender who probably served every one of you. We *will* get to the bottom of this, I promise. Two murders since you are guests on *my Contadora Island.* How can this be?" he asked the rhetorical question. "I have your passports and as I clear each of you, I will return them. We will call you by your room numbers and question you here. No one goes anywhere today until we have spoken to you."

The room held an ominous quiet until a whisper grew to indistinct chattering and spread from table to table like a light wind that blows burning embers across the field, igniting one bush and one tree at a time.

"Oh my God!" Liza gasped. "Basil, this isn't good." She whispered; "I know the paper Felix handed Rachel and she in turn handed to you was not Felix giving her his number so she could call him. Look at me! That is bullshit! What the hell is going on?"

"Quiet down! We don't want to draw the Commandant's suspicion." Before Basil could form another answer, the officer controlling the microphone called their room number. Both Basil and Liza rose, not having a choice. An officer escorted them into the manager's office. They had discussed and rehearsed a thousand times under the cloud of darkness, where they were and what they did on the night someone murdered Agent Henry Bradshaw. Their answers were; there could be no room for error. They knew of coerced false confessions used by foreign police. Basil saw it many times in Europe. However, they had not had time to rehearse where they were *this* day and night. No one had prior notice before the police questioned them. Score for the ponderous Commandant!

"Ah, yes. Elizabetta Dorsett and *Dr.* Basil Caprio," the Commandant greeted.

"Let's get on with it, if you don't mind," Basil directed the Commandant so he couldn't use his charm to relax them into a nonresistant state of mind. Basil was too smart for that. He knew how to manipulate the minds of others. Liza was banking on it.

"Alright then, go ahead tell me your whereabouts four days ago?" Zapata asked.

"Where we always are... either at the hotel, in town shopping and, of course, at The Red Rum Lounge in the evening," Basil responded. "I don't recall the day you had us brought to your headquarters. It could have been that day, or the day after our visit with you we went into town. We shopped, went back to the hotel to get ready for the evening at the Red Rum Lounge."

"Did anyone see you in town?" Zapata questioned.

"Yes, I had to exchange money at the bank. We exchanged pleasantries with the bank manager. It was brief, just business. Then, as I said, we came back."

"Señor Montebello?" he questioned, not giving Basil a moment to answer. "I will see him later. You may go... for now."

Back in their room, Basil reassured Liza. "You see? He has nothing. These are not Interpol police."

"What about the bank manager, Montebello? What will he tell Zapata?"

"Remember the C-notes he got? What do you think they're for? Señor Montebello may seem like a buffoon, but he is a clever man."

"Clever enough to want more of what he knows is in the bank book?"

"You should slip him the hundred while he's looking down your dress. He knows what's good for him."

Honesty, loyalty, and trust...

CHAPTER 32

"I'm tired of Zapata's bullshit, Basil. Maybe we should cut our time here and get the fuck off Contadora Island. Get out of Panama altogether."

"He's fishing, Liza. He isn't making progress, don't you see? Just like that fella on the boat said, he's grasping at straws. He's gaslighting. There's a lack of hard evidence surrounding the murders. That's hindering his progress or he would make an arrest. Leaving now would not be a smart idea. The Commandant would chase us, thinking we are his suspects. Adding to that; how can we leave when he still has our passports?"

"My God! It's such a short time that we're here and," she swept her hand around the room, "all of this. It's a lot to process. Two murders, meeting super star Rachel Kazz, surrendering to you. Okay, we can't be suspects, as you say." Her anxiety made her restless. "Do you have any more calm-me-down pills? They work fast and relax me."

"Here," Basil agreed, handing her what she asked for.

"What are these?"

"The medical term is Spirobarbital, if that makes you feel better to know."

"I'll ask you next time for spiro. It'll be our code name."

Basil knew how the drug worked: calmed the nervous system and its hypnotic and sedative effect. He also knew it had the potential to abuse the human system. At this moment, he accommodated Liza's request so she would not interfere with extracting one million dollars from Panama. They would help her get lost in his morass of misconception and explanations. Basil thought for a moment—*How much can she comprehend? How much information can she take? How far can I trust her? I want her to believe in me, but how honest can I be? What will she do if she finds out?*

"That's better," Liza sighed. "I can think better. Let's talk about leaving with our money. We can start the life we spoke about. You said yourself we may go back to New York, or maybe—Italy or Canada. All I want Basil is for us to do this together. You said you would help me get my life's dream, my five-star restaurant."

"Do you want to be a part of that---my dream? You can continue your practice and I my restaurant. We can have wonderful lives. You said..." She stopped, giving him a squinty-eyed look, "or were you saying these things just to get into my pants?" Liza knew what men wanted from her. She was the envy of the other girls as a teenager since the boys gravitated to her first, just like the other men in her life.

"Liza, please. You are saying things you'll regret later. You know how I feel about you. I want to share in your dream. I'm so happy I'm in your life. Why would I take you to the bank and add you to the accounts if I did not want to share with you?"

CHAPTER 33

"Basil, I did not forget the bullshit story you and Rachel gave me about the note. You lied. Why?"

"I did not want you to get upset, knowing that the person looking for me was here."

"Are you fucking kidding me? Why? Why would you do that? We agreed to be honest and trust each other. I want to know if you are in danger."

"This all happened before we made our promise. Felix knew of our past relationship, mine and Rachel's. He didn't know it was a professional one only. He conjured what he wanted to in his mind. We let him. Agent Bradshaw gave Felix grief. He described me, threw his weight around, used his credentials, and threatened Felix. Bradshaw took a shot that Felix had a police record and had an arrest warrant out on him. He thought Felix was from Madrid. Bradshaw was working on a hunch, and he was on the right track. Close, but no cigar. The thing is Felix had an arrest warrant, but it is from Morocco. He was French, not Spanish. Bradshaw's long shot spooked Felix so, he warned me. He knew I'd pay for information. He recognized me from Bradshaw's picture."

"I'm not following. Why would a U.S. Marshal be looking for you, and why would he try baiting me against you? You know, Basil, when I went to school one plus one always equaled two. This is not adding up... at all. If I try to add everything together, it does not add up to two. I bet it doesn't to you either, does it?"

"I understand your concern and you said it yourself. Agent Bradshaw was dirty. Montebello believed the hundred grand in the box was for a drug bust the agent was working or some big case. It wasn't. That was his dirty money from the shake downs he hid."

"Is your money, our money, dirty, Basil?"

"No!" He was emphatic. "No! I earned that million bucks. I love you. I want to share it with you. I want to share my *life* with you. Liza, please trust me. Commandant Zapata wants to put these murders to rest and maybe get another commendation."

"Oh my God!" Liza couldn't hold back.

"What! Oh my God, what?"

"You said you love me." Tears rolling down her cheeks, she walked into his arms.

"I do. I love you." Swallowing the lump in his throat, he realized he couldn't retract those words.

"I believe I do too---love you, Basil." *I never said that to any man, only to Calvin.*

"We can't let Zapata bamboozle us. We can't stay here indefinitely either. We need to have a plan in case this drags on. We have lives back in New York. Now that Agent Bradshaw is dead, and he was the one taunting me and looking for you, there is nothing more to run from."

"I understand why you feel that way. If Bradshaw was a dirty agent, that's how he knew I had money that Sylvia's father wants back. At first, they thought it was only a few thousand dollars, but Sylvia took one million dollars from the trust set up for her by her father. She felt I helped her so much, I deserved it. And it was hers to do what she wanted,"

Basil reasoned. "She has plenty more. Two Ton Paulie did not agree. He wanted that money back in her trust. He felt one million was outrageous for saving his daughter from her demons. The money was her way of getting back at her father. She wanted no part of it. Bradshaw must have found out about my payoff and wanted hush money. In return, he would not tell Sylvia's father where I was. I told you this from my meeting with him at the Tiki bar. Maybe Bradshaw killed Felix. I don't know. I'm not a detective; I'm a psychiatrist."

"Then you figure out what Commandant Zapata's brain is thinking."

"It doesn't work that way, Liza. I'm not a psychic or mind reader. I treat mental disorders."

"Well, if you ask me, Zapata has a mental disorder. I'm sorry. I'm just stressed out about all this. I need time to sort it all out. I'm still unclear about some things."

"I'm not unclear on what I said...." With a slight hesitation, Basil repeated, "I... I love you."

Liza silently considered his declaration of love. *He says he loves me, and he's glad he's in my life. What about me? Why didn't he say that he's glad I'm in his life? Isn't there a difference?*

CHAPTER 34

"I suspect Señor Montebello's loyalty. We've got to cement our relationship with him so he doesn't double cross us. Commandant Zapata and Montebello are cut from the same cloth just as we are. Who knows? They may even be cousins. This place has more consonants than vowels. We must have him in the palms of our hands so he will deliver what and when we want, don't you agree? Basil!" She raised her voice to get his attention; his glare was somewhere else.

"Yes, I agree. I want to fortify his trust and I want to be sure *we* agree. That is important to me, Liza. Is it not for you?" he asked.

"Oh. Basil! You of little faith. Don't turn into a *doubting Thomas*. You should question why Zapata wants to pin these murders on someone from the hotel, not on my feelings and commitment to you."

She had feelings for him, but *I also have feelings for one million dollars.* What Basil said to her, 'I'm glad I'm in your life,' not I'm glad you're in my life, cried out to Liza. *There is a difference!*

"It sounds like you have something in mind. Do you?" Basil asked.

"I may, I may not. I think we should meet Rachel as much as we can while she is here. I love how her fans trip over themselves, wanting to know who you and I are."

"The question is, are any celebrities or their fans any different from you and me? The way the mind works, it is easy for *normal* people to elevate celebrities. If one feels something missing inside, the brain naturally looks outside for compensation. This is because one has unmet needs. We all have unmet needs; don't you agree, Liza?"

"Thank you for bringing that out, Basil, with your psychoanalysis," Liza answered.

"I'm there too. I told you about my childhood. All it means is that some people do not realize what they are missing inside, so they look up to other people who display the characteristics they want and haven't yet developed, but they fear trying to get them. In their mind, celebrities possess more power and control than people without celebrity status. So lies the infatuation of Rachel's fans with us. Isn't it gratifying to be on the receiving side, Liza?"

"Oh, Basil, you can't imagine." Liza slurred her words as her eyes grew heavy. She fell into a drugged sleep from the spiro Basil gave her.

"You must trust and believe in people, or life becomes impossible." Anton Chekhov

CHAPTER 35

The more Basil thought of Liza's allegory of the man twisting the chicken's neck to get on the bus, the more fascinated he became with it. At the time he felt it was just a story because the bus they were riding on reminded her of a similar ride with Calvin—*No more chicken.*

He took advantage of Liza's stupor and made a telephone call before he left the room. Hiring a taxi, the driver took him to a small outdoor café on the same street where he and Liza caught the boat to Commandant Zapata's Headquarters. He approached a solitary man, sipping espresso.

"Ah, Alejandro, Saludo's mi amigo de españa," Basil greeted his contact from Spain. He tried to recall his limited Spanish from the required course at Sapienza University. *Close enough.*

"Saludo's Basil." Alejandro stood to greet him in the European manner. "I did not know we would pass each other coming and going to Commandant Zapata's Headquarters."

"Yes, he is questioning everyone from the hotel. I did not know you were staying there," Basil said. *How fucking stupid are you?* "I am grateful for the passports and the information, Alejandro. I have your money right here." He tapped the breast pocket of his jacket. "Can I order you anything? I will have an espresso; however, with a little Anisette."

Alejandro nodded his approval. "The waiters are slow here."

"As in Spain."

"No, thank you. I have my own," he told the waiter. Basil tipped the liqueur from his pocket flask. After sipping from the small cup, special for the strong, black coffee, Basil asked, "Alejandro, do you know of Plato's quotes?"

"I don't know Plato or his friends." He stared at Basil with furrowed eyebrows. "I know I need to get paid for my services and high tail it out of here. We could have met at the hotel."

"Yes, but that would put too many eyes on us. First, let me tell you about Plato and why I like him. He was an Athenian philosopher and a pivotal figure in the history of Ancient Greece. He was an innovator, like you, Alejandro. You are a magnificent innovator, an artist. Plato spoke of three main human behaviors. In my psychiatrist education, I studied him. Let me tell you."

"Do I really care, Basil?"

"I believe you will, my friend. Let me explain why I'm paying you."

"I know why. You're paying me for the contact I gave you in Barcelona and for making those passports for you and your lady *friend*." He gave Basil a vulgar gesture of them fucking.

"That is correct, my friend. You are like Michelangelo, an exceptional artist, and equally good at hand gestures. And the passports look genuine. I like to philosophize as Plato did. I realized why you do what you do and do it so well. Yes, I'm paying you for the information and service you rendered. However, you do this service because of the human behaviors Plato spoke about—emotion, desire, and the third is knowledge."

"What's your fucking point? I have a plane to catch," Alejandro said, a little edgy.

"Collect yourself. You are in too much of a hurry. You should enjoy the fruits of your labor; you are an artist. To continue, this will be a life lesson for you, my friend. Zeus was a mythical Greek God of the sky. He was the King of the Gods of Mount Olympus. He influenced the natural law and order of the cosmos, but he had no control over the fate of humans. Zeus was a God Plato looked up to. So, let me explain what Plato meant. Your emotion led you to desire a lot of money, no?" Basil asked rhetorically. "Yes, it did," answering for Alejandro. "Again, I have it here," tapping his breast pocket. "But to get the money you desire, the desire created from your emotion, both your emotion and your desire needed a great deal of knowledge to produce what I needed—information and passports. With that knowledge came power, Alejandro."

"Yeah, so what? Power is a good thing. Look at the power Commandant Zapata wields. His will controls who goes and who stays. He has everyone's passports." Alejandro sneered. "He can have mine; I've got plenty. I like that power."

"His power is weak compared to yours. Remember what I said. Zeus was a mythical Greek God of the sky. Plato knew him as the King of the Gods who influenced the natural law and order of the cosmos; however, he had no control over the fates."

"What fates," asked Alejandro?

"The fate of mankind: yours, mine, and Commandant Zapata's. The measure of a man is what you do with that power that is now yours. How will fate have you use the power you hold in your hand? You know who I am and where I've been, along with the counterfeit passports you made for me."

"Basil, if that is in fact your name, I don't give a shit what you do, who you are, where you go or who you do anything with. All I know is I rendered a service for professional counterfeit passports and information."

"Ah, yes, you did, Alejandro. I see you're a man who does not appreciate Greek mythology. Such a shame. However, I believe you will come to know what I'm speaking of. A man such as you realizes there's no security in being a criminal and no security in our fate as Plato philosophized. And now I shall pay you." Basil reached inside his suit jacket and pulled out an envelope. Standing, he said, "I will leave it on the table for you."

Alejandro looked puzzled, not caring about Basil's gibberish. He cared only for his money, but to portray trust for future business, he couldn't count it at the table. That would show mistrust.

Both men knew the European custom to greet and depart, the same for both men and women: the embrace, and the kiss on each cheek. While embracing, Basil stuck a hypodermic needle filled with enough iron dextran to kill a thoroughbred race horse into Alejandro's carotid artery. He whispered, "I couldn't chance what you would do with the power I gave you. My regrets, Alejandro. Like Zeus, Plato's God who had no control of human fate, this is your fate, your life's lesson. Rest in peace, my friend."

The injection's effect was immediate. Within minutes Alejandro's heart beat rapidly; he struggled to breathe and died. Slumping into Basil's arms, he gently sat Alejandro down to preserve his posture, setting the newspaper in front of him. Alejandro sat, head tilted down as if he was reading—

eyes wide in a vacant, stare. Basil picked up the envelope, took out a five-dollar bill, and placed it under the espresso cup, then walked away. *No more chicken.*

CHAPTER 36

"Where the hell have you been? You left no word — where I should meet you, what to do, go to dinner, or what. Nothing!" Liza shrilled. "I called the front desk to see if anyone saw you. Jesus Christ, Basil. You can't give me a spiro then leave without me knowing where the hell you are. What is it you don't get? I will not have our relationship rely on the blowing wind. Where were you?"

"I did not mean to upset you. You were sleeping. I thought I could just walk, maybe have a drink and think about us and our next move."

"Oh Basil, you always sound so considerate, and yet I'm getting the feeling you're lying. Why would I feel this way?"

"I don't know." The spiro still affected her senses. "Can we not take things for granted? We must build trust with one another. I trust you Liza, as I want you to trust me."

"You're holding back. There is something missing. You always have excuses and explanations of where you were — all too coincidental to the shit that is happening here on the island."

Basil could not keep his gaze off her; those taunting hazel eyes just oozed passion, but they seemed to hold a secret. Liza told him her life's story and opened herself to him with her dreams, but... *There's something about those eyes. They're not giving up their secrets.* His training and years of practice taught him how to read people. Knowing her vulnerability, she willingly accommodated him. He knew her responsiveness and manipulated her. Basil pressed against her so she could feel his desire.

Liza felt his warm skin and muscular physique. She tore open the blouse she slept in, feeling his breath move over her skin, bringing his lips to her perfect breasts. Her nipples peaked, hardened and so was he as he tugged her panties off.

"Let me show you how I trust you." She reached for him, taking what control he allowed her, guiding him where she wanted him. "Oh my God," she blurted, feeling lightheaded as her loins spasmed and tightened. She was seconds away, intoxicated on spiro, sex, the residue of red rums, and not least, what she allowed — submission. His kiss was ever so gentle as he eased from her. They lay in each other's arms.

Liza wanted more than romance and a good lay. She wanted financial security. This, however, was the fastest they'd ever made love. She wanted Basil to believe her emotions were involved, and everything else was of no consequence.

He was right. Liza's eyes held a secret, a secret she would not share.

"Just because I gave into you or you into me, we're not through with this discussion, Basil. You're not off the hook."

CHAPTER 37

Liza didn't want to become so enthralled with Basil and continued to rationalise her thoughts. She questioned them, and her decisions, but they confused her. *He's so thoughtful, genuine, so compelling. His love making, his tenderness... the money.* Trying to digest it all, the fucking money was all she could think about. *Can I spend my life with him and the money? I need that money — the God damn money! Can I believe in him? Can I trust him? He always worms his way out of situations with a viable excuse. Is every situation coincidental?* What gnawed at her the most was what Basil said... not once, but several times. *He's glad he's in my life, not he's glad I'm in his life.*

"You know, Liza, I'm thinking about going to Spain," derailing her thoughts. "I know you have time before you must return to work, but can you arrange more time off?"

Immediately, a red flag flashed. "What the fuck are you talking about? We have one million dollars in cash and one-hundred thousand dollars in a bank account, and you're asking me about returning to work? Are you insane? Why would I do that?" she asked, calmer than she felt. "You've said all along that we may have to go to another country and change our identities again and maybe another time. You said maybe we would not return to New York. Why wouldn't I accompany you to Spain?"

"Yes, forgive me, please. I'm not myself lately, and you aren't either. There's a lot riding on each other and our future—"

"Don't forget the money," Liza interrupted, "*our* money, and there's nothing wrong with my thinking. I wonder how you're thinking."

"Yes, yes, our money."

"Why can't we get the money out of here the same way you got it into Panama?"

"It's too complicated. I went to different countries and made wire transfers so I could get the money here. Panama is liberal, unconcerned with checking the source of money coming in or going out, particularly if you make a deposit and it stays in the bank for a while. With Zapata breathing down everyone's neck and scrutinizing every move, I could not wire that money from the bank without drawing suspicion. A wire transfer would wave a red flag."

"How long is *awhile* on deposit with the bank? And there's cash–one million in cash. We can get that out together. Leave the bank account with the other one- hundred thousand."

"No!" Liza drew back at Basil's harsh denial. Realizing her reaction, Basil tried to strategize. "You're correct. I don't know what I'm thinking, what I'm saying. We are both intelligent. Let's use our minds as one. What would be our best move? The banks like to have the money sit so they can use it, earn interest by lending it to other banks overnight. The banking business is complex."

"I'm not following you. We have nothing to hide. All we need to do is get our original passports back. Zapata can't keep them forever. We both know what's in the box at the bank, don't we?" Her smug smile irritated him. "And, why would you choose Spain? Of all places, why did you send the money to Panama? Why not New York or Italy?"

"Why… Why… Why! Didn't you hear anything I said?" he flared. "Two Ton Paulie Caserta is in New York and his contacts are in Italy. He has people in his pocket in both places — bankers, police, politicians. I thought I found a place to park the cash until I could move it. I never thought things would take shape here as they have. Panama was a simple place to hide money until now. You saw how excited Señor Montebello got each time I handed him a hundred-dollar bill. Panamanians love our United States dollar."

"Again, why Spain?" she continued, refusing to let Basil sidetrack her.

"It is beautiful, like Italy. It has a similar culture, food, art, and friendly people. Your five-star restaurant would be spectacular. The Mediterranean Sea is there. We would be close to France and Italy for holiday. Barcelona, yes, Barcelona it would be. It has mystique, just like Contadora Island with the ghosts of pirates protecting hidden treasures. Barcelona's legend attributes its foundation to Hercules. He searched for the Golden Fleece, traveling the Mediterranean in nine ships. Hercules lost one ship in a storm and he sets out to locate it. He finds the wrecked ship, but the crew was safe. They all were so taken by its beauty they named it Barca Nona, meaning Ninth Ship. It later became Barcelona."

"Trust me, Liza; you will fall in love with Barcelona. It's so much like our Italy. You will pick up the language. Think of your beautiful five-star restaurant with its magnificent view of the sea."

"That's fascinating, Basil, but I don't care about Hercules or the ghosts of Contadora Island as the brochure said. I'm here now. Yes, it has charm and romance. I see us and what happened in such a brief time. But Spain... Barcelona? What about our places in New York... my neighbor, Mrs. Philomena?"

"We will have enough money to keep our apartments and travel as you like. What happens to Mrs. Philomena when you're gone on holiday? Who looks after her and, as I recall, her cat, Boxy?"

"You're right. She relies on other neighbors while I'm gone. It's just a lot to accept, Basil. You understand, don't you?"

"I trust you and believe you—I believe *in* you. Liza, each day will never give you what the years turn out to be. This is today. What do you want from this day and every day coming until... death?"

"Wise men put their trust in ideas and not in circumstances." Ralph Waldo Emerson

CHAPTER 38

A crowd gathered to stare at the man sitting upright, mouth and eyes open, without moving. The waiter asked each time he passed if he wanted another espresso, without an answer or expression change—hours of an eerie downward stare. By the time Commandant Zapata arrived, rigor mortis had set in to Alejandro.

"Doctor, can you tell me what happened to this man?" Zapata asked of the Medical Examiner.

"He looks like he had a heart attack. Rigor has set, so it's been at least four, maybe six hours ago. I won't be able to tell until I get him on the table and open him up."

"How long will that be, Doctor?" Zapata wanted to know. "I need a report, soonest. My suspicion is if a person died with pain, fear, or they suffered torture or violence, their eyes and mouth would stay open to reveal a painful experience. Do you understand?"

"Commandant, whatever you wish. I know about that superstition. My autopsy will be accurate and I will confirm if your theory is correct."

"Yes, yes, I know your reports are accurate. Take the espresso, the cup, sugar too, Doctor. I want nothing left behind." Zapata turned to the crowd and shouted. "Everyone leave now; go about your business. Now! No more to see. Get all these people back," he ordered his officers. "Put up a barrier."

The M.E. lifted the cup, sniffed, before his men tagged and bagged it for testing.

"Commandant, this smells like whiskey. Ask the waiter if he ordered any liquor with his espresso, will you?"

"No!" the waiter replied.

"Okay, men, search him for a flask and identification. He must have something," commanded the M.E. "Empty all his pockets on the table. Let's have a look." All his belongings comprised identification, coins, U.S. currency bundled in a large rubber band, a small knife, a hotel key, a locker key, and the flask.

"Well, would you look at this?" Zapata picked up the hotel key. "He is or was staying at the Contadora Island Hotel. Ah! Now I remember. I questioned him at my office. His identification says he is Alejandro Otoya from Spain. It seems the hotel is again holding secrets. Doctor, now I need your report *rapido*."

"Yes, I will work on it immediately."

Handing what looked like a locker key to an officer, Zapata instructed him to find out what he could about the key. Selecting several officers, they drove to the Contadora Island Hotel.

The ride to the hotel was without incident. Zapata's officers knew his silence. It was an outward silence; they knew not to disturb the inner workings of his thoughts. They knew his ideas seemed to pan out. Commandant Zapata had two of his officers speak with the manager and desk clerks while he and the remaining officer went directly to the room number displayed on the key taken from Alejandro Otoya's body. Within minutes they swept the room and found nothing out of the ordinary, even after emptying his packed suitcase, ready for departure.

"Interesting," mumbled Zapata.

"Excuse me, Commandant, did you say something?" asked the officer.

"Yes. Why do you think he was ready to travel when I have all the passports? I have released none yet."

"I don't know Commandant. This is why you are in charge," replied the officer with diplomacy.

"Keep your eyes open and learn. Let us go to another room. Come with me."

"Ah! Commandant Zapata. This is or should I say is not a surprise," Basil said as he opened the door to the Commandant.

"I am sorry to disturb you and Mrs. Dorsett, Doctor. May I have a moment?"

"Yes. Come in."

Zapata stationed his officer outside the door. "Mrs. Dorsett?" he questioned with a suspicious look around the room.

"She is waiting for me in the dining room. Would you care to join us?" Basil extended the courteous invitation hesitantly.

"Thank you, no. This is a professional call. I would like your help."

"Of course, Commandant." *Christ, this could be our ticket out of here.*

"You being a psychiatrist, I would like your help in analyzing how people think… their behaviors and why they do some evil things they do."

"I'd be honored to be of service."

"Good. I will send for you the day after tomorrow. I am waiting for some information that I feel you can help with. Shall we say 10 a.m.?"

"Perfect. I'll be ready," Basil answered, suppressing the urge to push him out the door.

Turning, Zapata offered as an afterthought. "Mrs. Dorsett is welcome to come with you, if you wish. Good evening."

Basil rushed to the dining room. Liza would be impatient, unaware his brief discussion with the Commandant had caused him to be late.

"Basil you look like the cat that swallowed the canary," Liza suggested, annoyed with his tardiness.

"You will not believe this. Zapata came to our room. He wants me to help him."

"Help him. Are you crazy? Help him how?" she asked. "Why the hell would he want your help? C'mon, Basil. I smell a rat, a fucking Police Commandant rat. Maybe he was in with the dirty U.S. Marshal. He's flim-flaming you."

"Calm down. I think this is why he wants my help—"

"He doesn't want your help. He wants to set you up. He's a conniving son-of-a-bitch. You're a psychiatrist for Christ's sake, and you don't see through him? You said it yourself. He acts like a stumble bum, but he is very calculating."

"Let me go with this. I have an idea and I don't see what you're seeing. Maybe you're right. I know what I said. If I give him false cognitive narrative, he may buy it and it will lead him away from me, from us. We can get out of here with our original passports. Trust me. I know what I'm doing. I have an idea."

"You better. I don't like it, but for now I'll go along with you."

CHAPTER 39

The Red Rum lounge was buzzing as usual. Customers were stirring, loud indistinct chatter competed with glasses, dishes, and silverware rattling as everyone anticipated the headliner, Rachel Kazz.

"Ah-ha. Welcome, Basil and the lovely Liza. What can I get you? Let me see if I remember. Red Rums, correct? Yes, Felix's special as you pointed out to me."

"Yes. And if I remember, it's Julio, yes?"

"Señora, you are magnificent in memory and may I add—."

"No, Julio, you may not," Basil's curt response interrupted. Just do your job. Maybe you are familiar with the customers to a fault."

"I'm sorry if I offended you or your lady." Julio took a chance that Liza, being on vacation, might be interested in him. *You never know. Many women come to an exotic island for a little side action.*

"Your drinks are on me for the evening. Please, I did not mean any disrespect. Your table will be perfect. I'll be a moment."

"Wait!" Instructed Liza, halting Julio in his tracks, hoping she changed her mind.

"Yes?" questioning her command.

"What do you know about Felix?" she asked.

"Not much. They found him close to the beach. Everyone is asking, but the police are not saying. You know, holding back important information."

"Thank you. We'll be waiting."

Perfect it was. Julio set their table front row to the stage. Rachel could reach out and touch them.

"Basil, this is great. I don't think Julio meant any harm. Let's enjoy the evening and Rachel's show. Relax, please. Catch the waiter and order another drink."

"You don't understand as a man—"

"Oh, I think I do," Liza interrupted, "He bruised your ego, but Señor Montebello did not. Tell me the difference. Wait! I know. Montebello, we may need to get our money out quietly and swiftly. So, his looking down my dress, checking out my breasts was okay? Julio's comment was a direct hit against your manhood because you would not gain from it. Is that correct?"

"Liza, did you go to school for psychology? Jesus, Mary, and Joseph! I'm embarrassed to say you are right. How did you—"

"Jesus, Mary, and Joseph had nothing to do with it."

"Ladies and gentlemen, the star you've been waiting for… the sensational, the woman with the *razz-ma-tazz*, the divine Rachel Kazz." The Master of Ceremony's voice resounded in the lounge.

Rachel basked in the crowd's roar and standing applause that greeted her and consumed her entire being. The applause died. Rachel gave her pianist a nod, sounding the introduction to *For Sentimental Reasons*. The orchestra followed the downbeat.

Her style, her grace, her beauty enchanted Liza. She couldn't believe that Basil kept their relationship platonic, seeing the few times Rachel and he touched and her calling him 'Baby.' Liza reached for Basil's hand, pulling him close to her for a quick kiss, darting her eyes toward the stage to see if Rachel caught what she wanted her to see. It was perfect timing as Rachel sang the lyric, *I love you and you alone were meant for me.* What threw Liza was Rachel's wink of approval, not any gesture of jealousy. *Maybe it was so. Maybe they were never lovers. This dame's got class.*

Rachel's two-hour show seemed to last only fifteen minutes. She was so dynamic you couldn't imagine that much time slipped by. You could not help wanting more. Rachel always said, "You need a great opening and a fantastic close. The middle will take care of itself," and she was right. She came back for an encore that had everyone on their feet screaming and whistling with deafening applause.

She fulfilled her stage mantra. Leaning toward the audience, shaking hands as the grips brought bouquets of flowers to her from the crowd. She worked her way toward Basil and Liza, signaling them to come backstage with the tilt of her head. The night was young and there were a lot of Red Rums to consume.

CHAPTER 40

Returning to her routine ho-hum life of slinging Blue-Plate specials at the Crosstown Diner was far from Liza's thoughts, although she wondered about her neighbor, Mrs. Philomena and Boxy. *I know there are other neighbors to help. But I am the one that does most of the looking in. Maybe I should go back to what I did before going to France and meeting Calvin.* Slowly, Liza lifted her head from the pillow. She remembered a high school girlfriend paraphrasing an expression in Jewish meaning not to rattle the teacups in her head, so she moved with caution.

"Basil, where are you?" *Jesus! I don't know what will happen with me and Basil. It could work out, or maybe not! I have ideas and dreams I need to fulfill – the dreams Calvin and I had.*

"I'm right here." He handed her his hangover special.

"What is this?"

"It's hair of the dog! Drink it. You'll feel better."

"What the hell is in it? What is hair of the dog? It sounds nasty."

"It's an old remedy to cure the morning after drinking. It's just an expression. Drink up; It will help you."

Liza eyed the glass with suspicion, brought it to her nose and sniffed. No medicinal smell, so she took a small sip. "Hmm, not bad. It tastes great. I think we should change its name, maybe chasing the dog, or bark at the dog."

"I'm going down to get the newspaper and get us a table for breakfast. I had my 'chasing the dog,'" giving a bit of a chuckle. "I'll be waiting."

"Basil, I have to get ready. Wait for me." She took another sip of the concoction he made for her.

"Okay, I'll call for a table. Try to hurry."

Again, she thought of the money. *It's not just random circumstance that I'm here with Basil and one million dollars. I have to think of how to get this money out of here.*

The waiter escorted them to their table. Before he left, Basil asked him to please get him the morning paper, which he brought promptly.

"Oh shit!" Basil exclaimed, reading a story on the front page.

"What? What is it, Basil?" Liza asked with trepidation.

"A man died at some café near Zapata's headquarters. The reporter says he might have been drugged or poisoned. The victim was staying at this hotel. Jesus, Liza, this will be another arrow in Zapata's quiver to aim at someone in the hotel. He'll try to tie this in to the other murders because this man was a guest here. This is number three."

"When did it happen?"

Suspicion Always Haunts the Guilty Mind…Shakespeare

CHAPTER 41

"Ah, Doctor Caprio. I'm glad I caught you both here. Mrs. Dorsett," Zapata greeted her with a tip of his hat. "Do you remember my asking you for your help?"

"Commandant, please sit down, join us." Basil raised his hand for the waiter to bring coffee and menus.

Liza glared at him. *What the fuck are you doing?*

"Thank you, Doctor, Mrs. Dorsett." Zapata removed his hat. "I see you have the morning paper. I hoped to get to you before you read about the dead man at the café. Have you read it?" Zapata asked.

"Why no, I haven't yet," Basil tried not to glance at Liza, wanting Zapata to disclose his thinking.

"At first we thought it just a heart attack. For such a young man, it was unfortunate. However, our medical examiner found his death suspicious."

"What does that mean, Commandant, suspicious?" Liza asked.

"I mean just that, Mrs. Dorsett. It seems someone gave him a substance, which our medical examiner found — Iron Dextran. He found a small puncture wound, just the size of a hypodermic needle. The killer injected the chemical into his neck. Our ME almost missed it until he discovered what killed him."

"What is Iron Dextran?" Liza asked.

"I'll let you answer, Doctor. I'm not schooled in medicine."

"You're doing fine, Commandant," growing suspicious of where this was going.

Zapata glanced at Liza, whose countenance was that of innocence while Basil's was not. "Iron Dextran is a medical treatment for an iron deficiency —"

Liza interrupted. "Maybe he was like a diabetic who measured their insulin wrong and took too much of it. Diabetics have done that, you know."

"Unlikely, Mrs. Dorsett," Zapata answered. "The dosage in his blood was enough to kill several men. This was murder number three on Contadora Island. I'm getting an obvious message that all three are linked together."

"Why do you think that, Commandant?" Basil asked, fishing for as much information as possible without drawing attention to himself.

"We found two keys on him. One to his room here at the hotel which we searched, and one to a locker at Tocumen Internacional Aeropuerto."

"Why would he have a key to a locker at the airport if he was staying at the hotel?" Liza asked.

"It's very simple, Mrs. Dorsett. We found a bag which many criminals use as a *'bolsa rāpida.'*"

Liza looked at Zapata with a question.

"Ah, *pardōneme* Señora. It is a quick get-a-way pack, known as a go bag. It contained incriminating information. This person had six passports, all with a blank space where photos should be. All had different names from six countries, twenty-five thousand dollars in U.S. currency, a plane ticket, a gun, and a book with writing in it that appears to be coded notes," stated Zapata.

Did Basil know this man? Six fake passports...like my Liza Caprio passport?

That look on Liza's face...she's thinking of the fake passports in the bank box. Why is the Commandant sharing so much information? Damn him!

Well versed in psychological profiling, Basil tried to interject reverse psychology on the Commandant. "Maybe Commandant, this man—"

Zapata interrupted. "Alejandro Otoya was his name."

"I would think it still is his name, wouldn't you Commandant?" Not waiting for an answer, Basil continued. "It appears Señor Otoya was conducting some criminal activity and met someone at the café. Perhaps this Otoya killed the U.S. Marshal and the bartender, Felix, for whatever reason. Maybe a professional hit man killed Otoya to be sure whoever is behind all this can't be traced. Maybe he double crossed this person, and he paid the consequences."

"Ah, Doctor Caprio, that is quite a theory. You can work as a detective."

"No, thank you. I'm fine being a psychiatrist. You asked for my help the other day. Is this what you want me to help you with?"

"Doctor?" Questioned Zapata.

"You asked me to help you try to figure the mind of a criminal and why they do the things they do, correct?"

"Yes, yes. That was before this incident. But maybe you can help here too," Zapata suggested.

Basil got more wary. "Any way I can," *This man is no bumbling idiot. He's got me in his periscope.* Again, he planned. *If I offer to look at this codebook, he will get the notion that I want to know what's in it.*

"Good, as we left off before, I will send for you tomorrow. Mrs. Dorsett, you are welcome to join us. Have a pleasant day." Zapata replaced his hat at a precise angle and stood.

"You're welcome to stay and have breakfast, Commandant," Basil offered.

"Thank you, but no. I have many, many things to sort out. I will see you tomorrow." He tipped the brim of his hat to Liza.

CHAPTER 42

"Basil, I'm nervous and your face is telling me the same story. Why would that be?" Liza asked, her voice stern.

"Let's think for a moment," Basil answered with sarcasm. "Why the hell wouldn't I be nervous? Zapata is using every trick in the book to get to me. He thinks I had something to do with all three murders or knows what's going on. He's trying to prove I'm involved in some way."

"Why would he think you are guilty? *Are* you guilty in any way?" Liza tried to pin Basil to the wall using unanswered dialog. He was a master at skirting the issues at hand. They sipped their coffee, Basil with unease.

"What do you think he will ask your help with?" Liza asked.

"Likely the same things the police have called on my expertise before, but I don't think Zapata's questioning will be routine. He's going for a brass ring on the merry-go-round."

"Let's play this out, Basil. I'll be Zapata, and I'll ask you some things. How's that?" Liza suggested, sarcasm and motive in mind.

"I don't know, Liza. You may work for Zapata," Basil answered with a smirk and a chuckle.

"Is that how a psychiatrist's mind works? When a patient makes a statement, you ask, why do you think that, or how do you feel about that?"

"Liza, are you sure you didn't go to University and study to be a psychiatrist? Maybe you were a patient at one time, perhaps after Calvin's death? You can talk to me, you know.

We'll have doctor-patient privilege, then we'll have the privilege of making love. How does that sound?"

"How does what sound?" Liza answered with tension. "It sounds as if you want to skirt the issue as usual. That's what it sounds like to me."

"Okay, go ahead, Commandant Zapata, fire away!"

CHAPTER 43

"Good morning, Doctor and Mrs. Dorsett. Thank you for coming."

Liza smiled. *Like we had a choice if we wanted to dispel your suspicions.*

"I'm stumped as to the entire goings on concerning these deaths on my island. I'm hoping, Doctor, that you'll help me understand why a person can do such horrible things to other human beings. It is mystifying: three murders only weeks apart. Never in all my years has this happened."

"Doctor, let me tap into your education at University. The autopsy results show that a lethal injection of Iron Dextran poisoned Señor Otoya. In simpler terms, someone murdered him." Zapata glanced at Liza to see her reaction. "We spoke about this and you had knowledge of the drug as a doctor. We know the other two murders, Agent Bradshaw and Felix, were different circumstances. A gunshot killed Agent Bradshaw—"

"Felix was strangled," Basil said.

Stunned, Liza turned to Basil with a quizzical expression. Zapata had not disclosed how Felix died, but he showed them the photo of Bradshaw with a bullet hole in his forehead.

"Doctor," Zapata questioned, "How do you know? We did not release that information to the public. How did you come up with that deduction?"

"You mentioned, Commandant, that both seemed to be what you labeled a 'professional hit.' Despite his error, Basil had to respond without hesitation. "Since you used the photo of Agent Bradshaw with a bullet in his head for shock value to see our reactions, I assumed you would have showed a photo of Felix if that was the method used in his demise. You did not. I could only assume Felix was strangled. I assume you did not show us a photo because his face would be distorted, his eyes popping out of his head. He was most likely strangled with a garrote. Am I correct, Commandant?"

"That is correct. I did not want to upset anyone," turning to Liza, he dipped his head. "Death can be gruesome, don't you agree?"

"Yes, I do." Basil did not inform Zapata he had helped the police on other matters of murder multiple times before. He was relieved that Liza insisted they play out potential scenarios Zapata might conjure.

"What's a garrote," Liza asked.

"A device used to strangle someone… a wire or some strong fabric… like a nylon stocking. The garrote could have handles on each end or be long enough to wrap around an assailant's hands to prevent it from slipping. Nylons have only been around the last few years. Is that correct, Doctor?" Zapata asked.

"Yes. During my studies, I saw victims at University, Commandant. They were not pleasant to see, not that any victim of a crime is. With strangulation, blood flow to the brain stops, teeth injure the lips, eyes bulge, and the victim loses control of bodily functions."

"Oh my God," Liza blurted out in horror, paling at such an image.

Liza's sudden outburst did not jar Zapata. He continued the session as smooth as butter melting on a sizzling steak. "So, Doctor, tell me your thoughts."

Liza shifted in her chair, getting more uncomfortable. She had not anticipated this part of his interrogation... purposely inviting her reaction to see how they would interact with one another.

Basil knew Zapata's ploy, police methods, and the workings of the criminal mind from helping solve crimes in Italy and New York. He would have to be vigilant and not show any guilt to further arouse the suspicion Zapata tried to camouflage.

"Basil leaned forward, looking Zapata straight in the eye, knowing how to answer and not draw suspicion to himself or Liza. "Commandant, I think someone strangled Felix. And as you said, 'by a professional hit man' or a man trained in the military. Most perpetrators would not know about a garrote or its purpose. They would probably just choke the person. However, a professional hit man or law enforcement would know what a garrote is, how to make one, and use it. Like any professionals in his field of endeavor, they would know their craft. Only this professional's craft is killing people."

Pausing, Basil looked thoughtful. "Do you think the man that was poisoned and the United States Marshal are connected with poor Felix?"

"This is why I've asked you here to help me resolve that. Contadora Island is a beautiful tourist destination. Why would these three, who are so different, be killed here of all places, within days of each other? It is reasonable to me to assume they are connected. What are your thoughts, Doctor? What kind of mind works that way? Do you see a connection?"

"I'm not a detective. I'm a psychiatrist, remember?"

"Yes, I do. And you can also dispense medications. So, you have many attributes to offer."

This son-of-a-bitch is getting on my nerves. Basil's unease escalated. "It seems reasonable that some weird circumstance connects them—a U.S. marshal, a bartender and a criminal, but I could not offer you a reason. I *can* help you with the mind of a psychopath."

"And that is, Doctor?" asked Zapata.

"The psychopath knows what he or she is doing is wrong, but does not care. They form no emotional attachments. Some have charming personalities. Psychopaths are manipulative, often well educated, and easily earn people's trust. They are organized, intelligent people who leave few or no clues. Usually, he or *she* does not kill just for the thrill. They justify their kill, such as financial gain. So, they reason if they did not kill a particular person, they would be in jeopardy from whatever they did or will do, and believe the victim might incriminate or harm him or her. They don't want to face any consequences, so they see murder as the easy alternative."

"So, Doctor, do you think this was for financial gain? I can see that with Agent Bradshaw since we found all that cash in his box in the bank. We feel he was a dirty agent, likely taking bribes, and involved in criminal activity. He had a book with notes too."

"Cash, and a book with notes? How much cash? What notes?" Basil asked, implacable and steady in his tone, asking although he already knew about the cash.

"The same with Señor Alejandro Otoya," Zapata moved to another victim without answering. "We located the airport locker with the bag stashed inside. He had a wad of cash and several passports. He, too, had a book with notes. We are comparing them to see if they match. Those two may have done business together, and it did not go the way someone expected, but Felix does not seem to fit. We found nothing incriminating in his home. There were no bankbooks, or keys to lockers, or bank boxes, or a notebook. He lived a simple life like a typical young man… messy place, empty refrigerator except for beer, rum, and stale food. We tore his place apart and found nothing. Felix does not fit into this professional hit for financial gain scenario. I hoped you could shed some light on this, Doctor."

"Felix could have found out something about these men. Bartenders pick up on everyone's conversations. Maybe he waited on these two men at the bar. He served the Tiki bar in the day and the inside lounge in the evening. He was personable, as I remember, and had an engaging personality. Don't you agree, Liza?" Basil tried to get her involved to divert Zapata's suspicion.

"Yes, Felix was a pleasant, engaging young man. I saw him flowing in and out of conversations—you know, listening, not showing his interest, talking only when he needed to. Felix's death is so sad, not that the other two men aren't, but it seems from what I've heard, Commandant, the other two were criminals. 'Live by the sword, die by the sword'… that sort of thing," Liza chimed in to support Basil's plea.

"Ah yes. The book of Matthew. I see your point, Mrs. Dorsett, and a good one, but that still leaves Felix a murder victim. Why him? There's no evidence to tie him to the other two murders. I hope the notes in the books we found will help us," Zapata said.

"Commandant, if it would help, I will look at those notes. I may recognize something as to the criminal psychopath's mind." He hoped Zapata would agree and he would find something to lift Zapata's suspicion from him and Liza.

"I will keep you informed of our progress. You have been most helpful, Doctor. This has been an interesting session. I am now convinced that the killer is a professional, and Felix might have been in the wrong place at the wrong time... *unless* these books reveal something different. And, as you said, who and why is this killer getting paid to kill people on *my island*? The killer is still at large. All the airports are on high alert. The person who killed Señor Otoya is still here, somewhere between Contadora Island and the mainland. Thank you both. I will provide a ride for you to wherever you would like to go."

CHAPTER 44

"Basil, time is running out. I have to reach out to my boss and let him know I'm not coming back to work. I should get in touch with my neighbors too, so they'll look in on Mrs. Philomena and Boxy."

"Who and what is Boxy?" Basil inquired.

Liza looked at Basil, recognizing he was out of touch with who was important to her. "Mrs. Philomena, my elderly widowed neighbor and Boxy is her cat, remember?" She reminded him with annoyance.

"Oh, yes, yes. I was thinking of the Commandant. He is snooping around too much. I've seen this happen before on police matters. They give you a little information and see what you come up with. They want to see if you are legitimate in your profession and what you can offer them. They've used me, but I've proved how good I am in connecting with the mind of a psychopath. We need a maneuver to get our original passports returned to us so we can get off this island. I don't know about you, but I've had enough of it."

"Basil, if we are going to Spain, and we have other passports in the bank box, why would we have to wait to get what Zapata is holding back? And why do you say Zapata is snooping around too much?" Liza saw the tension in Basil's face. "Shit! Do you suspect he thinks we are involved in all of this? Why would he think that? You need to convince him that is preposterous. We need to get on with our lives. Has he returned *any* passports? I've seen people checking out of the hotel. I'll take a shower and get ready for dinner. We'll catch another Rachel show. I like her."

"Me too. I'll be right behind you." *You may never get in touch with your past.*

"Basil, have you seen my nylons?" Liza called out,

"I saw them hanging over the shower bar to dry."

"I thought so, but they're not here. Will you look in my drawer, please?"

Basil walked into the bathroom, pulling the shower curtain aside. He stepped in to join Liza, asking for the soap. "Turn around, let me wash your back. I found your nylons in your drawer."

"That's another pair. Where are the ones I had drying?"

"Maybe the housekeeper snagged them," Basil shrugged. "You know how hard it is to get such luxuries here."

"Maybe we should lock things in our luggage." She dismissed the missing stockings, seeing Basil next to her. "Don't forget, I have another side to wash," she murmured, turning to kiss him and reaching for what he had ready for her.

Truth and communication are hard to come by...

CHAPTER 45

Rachel's show was winding down on the island. Soon she would be off to New York. Liza's mind raced. *Maybe we could be part of Rachel's troop and escape this island debacle.* She still had questions and there were too many questionable circumstances to ignore the note Felix handed Rachel who passed it to Basil. The first explanation Basil gave her was bullshit, then he explained. Her mind was spinning, and she hadn't had a drink. She wanted to believe Basil—Agent Bradshaw was shaking him down so he wouldn't tell Two Ton Paulie Caserta where Basil and his money were. Caserta wanted it all put back into his daughter's trust. *Why did Rachel lie about the note? Why didn't Felix hand it to Basil?*

"Liza, are you okay? Julio is waiting for your order," Basil asked.

"You know what we drink. I will have a prime rib, medium, nothing else, okay Basil?" Liza spoke with an insolent stare.

"I'll have the same, Julio, please, with our Red Rums." He was more courteous.

"Fuck you," Liza glared at Basil. With a suppressed grin, Julio hurried away.

"Where is that coming from? Are we arguing? It may be our first genuine one. We've had some differences of opinion, but not a lover's quarrel. I like it. It's healthy… and exciting. Fuck you too for whatever reason you said it to me."

"Basil, we are in the middle of a fucking murder investigation, three to be exact. Don't you see how Zapata is drawing you into this? Now, by association, me with you?

"No, I don't. I have his number. Zapata is trying to be coy. I will give him all the information he will accept about how a killer's mind works. Stop worrying, please. I will help him and we will get our original passports returned, I promise. You cannot let him see that he rattled you. This is what the police look for in interrogations. They apply suspicions until the guilty conscience takes over and... Voila! [9] He gets a confession. Besides, we have done nothing wrong and have nothing to hide. *We* have not committed murder. Remember, my Liza, you agreed from the onset you are in this with me, one hundred percent, all the way. You have access to one million dollars and the bank account with another hundred thousand in it. Did you forget?" asking a rhetorical question.

No. I did not forget, and I sure as hell didn't forget all that money. "Basil, you know what I said and what I've committed. We've been over this. Why are you questioning me? I'll say it again. I'm with you. I'm all in, except for the caveat."

"What caveat?"

"The caveat of murder. Did you have anything to do with any of these murders, Basil? Don't lie to me. Some things that happen in life just happen; you know—for a reason. That dirty Agent Bradshaw deserved what he got. He was a first-rate criminal, a douche bag, trying to put the fear of God in me with his telephone calls. I told you. And shaking you down? Imagine, he thought he would take our money, just

---

[9] Voila is French for "Wah-Lah.

like that," snapping her fingers. "He got what he deserved, that dirty bastard."

Her diatribe shook Basil—like a man who just received the bolt of electricity thrown from the switch connected to the electric chair at Sing Sing Prison. *I can't believe what I just heard. Maybe there is hope for this woman. A few more good lays and I just may tell her the ultimate ride she's in for.*

Waiters stopped serving dinner and more Red Rums appeared and appeared and appeared. Rachel's show was as spectacular as the first time Liza heard her. She recalled Felix's words. 'Her voice is pure as the driven snow that matches her heart. She is magnificent, far above Savannah, our dinner entertainment.' *That she is, and poor Felix, dead!*

It was close to an hour before Rachel was able to make it to their table, through milling fans seeking pictures and autographs. She knew her public brought her to where she was and where she was going. She would never disregard them. The crowd subsided, but once in a while a solitary fan approached, meekly presenting a menu for her to autograph.

The dancing orchestra took center stage, quieting the crowd. Then they knew they would have time to themselves.

Liza broke tonight's awkward silence. "I'm still baffled by Felix's note, supposedly asking you, Rachel, for your number. That was a lie! You said you didn't want to let Felix down, so you gave it to Basil to discourage Felix. We all know, the note said. *He's here.* What the fuck did that mean, *He's here*? It sure wasn't Felix asking you for your number. Suddenly, a man turns up dead! Did that mean Bradshaw, the dirty agent, was here? How did Felix know that? How are you, Basil and Felix involved in this, Rachel? The note went from Felix to you and to Basil. Now Felix and Agent Bradshaw are dead. How the fuck does that work?"

"Liza, all I know is Felix asked me to hand that note to Basil. I had no idea what it said or what it was for. It seemed the thing to do. We had a capacity crowd; Felix was busy and could not reach Basil. He was next to me, if you'll recall. Felix said, 'Pass this to Basil, will you?' I thought nothing of it. I heard my cue for the show to start and reacted to the situation at hand. It's that simple. I went on stage. Why are you asking?

"You said that Felix wanted your number. That was not the note. You lied. It said; *He's here*. Now the agent and Felix are dead… murdered. And there's a third murder."

"My God!" Rachel exclaimed. "What? What third murder? What are you saying, Liza?"

"Someone injected a man with an overdose of some chemical."

"Oh no, I heard nothing about that. When? Who?" she asked.

"That's what Commandant Zapata asked. He's seeking the truth behind it all, as I am—now. Rachel, the note?" Liza asked with dogged determination.

"Yes, the note. I told you, Liza," Rachel retorted. "I did not read the note. I told you it was Felix asking for my number for this reason. If it ever came to question, as now, I thought it would be a simple explanation. Now I see I was wrong. I'm sorry. I made that story up, not knowing what was in the note. What I've witnessed between you and Basil seemed genuine. For all I knew, the note was a list of island hookers. I did not want to get involved, although I did by passing the note to Basil. I should have told him to give it to Basil himself. I'm sorry, Liza. That's the truth."

"Yes, Rachel, I believe you with Basil's explanation of Felix being blackmailed by Agent Bradshaw. I see that now.

The truth is a hard mirror to face. I just wanted to hear it from you."

"That bastard agent was shaking you down, Basil? Why?" Rachel asked, not showing the hand she held. "I don't understand."

Basil glared at Liza and held it for a moment before he focused on Rachel to see her reaction to what Liza just spewed. His countenance spoke volumes as to the faux pas Liza just committed.

"It's a long story, Rachel," Basil said. "It is one of my patients. The family accused me of stealing a sizeable sum of money from them and wants it back. The agent tracked me here and wanted a cut of the money to say he couldn't find me."

"Well, did you take money from them, Basil?" Rachel's casual question interested Liza.

"No!" Basil answered.

"Then you have nothing to worry about," Liza said.

"I second that, Liza. I like your candor and tenacity. Basil, you have quite a woman by your side. You better not fuck this up," Rachel said with sincerity.

Liza smiled. "Thank you, Rachel."

"Do you hear me and understand what I'm saying, Basil?" Rachel pursued, hoping she had distracted Liza and her questions about the note would end.

"I do. I really do," Basil answered as he searched his soul.

CHAPTER 46

The night's tension eased and continued on a cheerful note, lasting to the wee hours of the morning. The bar did not have a closing time as regulations demanded in the States. A few musicians stayed to jam and wind down from the crowd pumping them up with an entertainer's adrenaline. Basil, Liza, and Rachel continued to dance with one another, taking turns.

A small crowd lingered with them enchanted with Rachel's beauty, hoping to hear her sneak in a number or two, which she did. Rachel didn't care if there were two hundred in the room or only two people, she would sing. She said, "No matter how old I get or how many times I perform, the thunderous applause and the smell of the greasepaint will keep me going, not how much money I make, like so many other entertainers.[10]

Liza suspected a handsome, well-dressed man at a table nearby. She studied him covertly as he sat alone, facing their table. *Shit! Is this another man like Agent Bradshaw, trying to shake us down?*

"Liza, are you okay?" Rachel asked.

"That man sitting over there keeps looking toward us. He gives me a creeping sense of dread."

---

[10] The smell of the greasepaint (theatrical make-up) used by some stage performers, gave meaning to their performance. The thunderous applause, is self-explanatory.

"He's okay, Liza. He's from the record producers. I took your advice about a body guard and they agreed to have him and others when I get to the States as part of my contract. I don't even have to pay them. I owe you for that. Thank you. He's kinda handsome, don't you think?" Rachel asked.

"Don't go there, Rachel," Basil interjected. "It will only make trouble for you with the press and the paparazzi. Temptations come in many forms. I know the effect it will have on your career. As your former therapist, I advise you to keep it professional. Stay away from your bodyguard."

"I guess you're right, but it's such a shame, Look at him."

"I know I'm right. It would be taboo."

"You know, Basil; I'll need more therapy with all this success. I can feel it. Will you be up-to-it?"

Basil turned to see Liza's reaction. Seeing her nod her head in approval shocked him.

"We'll work something out, Rachel. I think you have time."

"It's late… or I should say early? I have several big days coming up—lawyers, producers, contracts—all that business stuff. You'll excuse me? It's been fun. I'll be around for about a week. Remember what I said, Basil," looking him in the eye before turning to Liza. "Good night," Rachel smiled, getting up to leave as her body guard rose in unison.

Basil and Liza strolled to their room, arm in arm, unconsciously loosening their clothes along the way.

CHAPTER 47

"Basil, I told you I need to reach out to my boss and my neighbors. They'll be alarmed if I don't come home on schedule. Someone has to look in on Mrs. Philomena and Boxy. I have to arrange for my mail too."

"You can't!"

"What! I have to. I can't just disappear. You probably made these arrangements before you left somehow, maybe with your secretary. That is my life in New York."

"You can't! Be reasonable, Liza. Any wire transfers, telephone calls, or outgoing mail will be monitored, and a report forwarded to the Commandant. Everyone's on notice. I'm sorry."

"How the hell would you know that? Is that just your supposition?"

"No, it's not. The Policia in Italy did those same things when I helped them sort out a killer's thought patterns. That's what got him caught. He was in Milan. I told them to set up surveillance for all banks and wire transfer outlets because he couldn't stay in one place and would need money to escape. It worked. He thought he could outsmart everyone. He instructed his cousin in Abruzzi to call his brother in New York and wire money out of his bank account in the Bronx. He wanted it wired to Rome so he could get out of Italy. He thought the Policia would not trace the different people and instructions. He even traveled over five-hundred miles to a wire depot in Rome. The Policia had every bank and wire depot known in Italy on alert for wire activity. As soon as the money arrived in Rome, the Policia were waiting for him. It did not end well. They shot and killed him."

"Jesus Christ! I have to figure out a way to get my messages out. Help me. I just can't sit here and do nothing. If I have to, I'll go to the bank and get one of those passports to leave. Everything...."

"Okay, okay," interrupted Basil. "I'll find a way for you to get a message to everyone you need to contact. Give me some time to put it together."

"Don't waste any time, Basil, I'm warning you."

CHAPTER 48

Basil's mind raced. *How am I going to get Liza's messages sent, knowing Zapata has all our communications tracked?*

"Liza, let's go, get ready."

"What? Where are we going?"

"We will walk into the lion's den itself, Commandant Zapata's Headquarters, and tell him we must send notifications stating that we are being held on an island controlled by the Panama military."

"What! Are you duzi botts, pazzo, crazy? He'll eat us alive. You're making *me* crazy with this idea."

"No! Listen. We'll confront him head on. Trust me. Let's go."

"You're a crazy man," Liza mumbled. "Why do I listen to you?"

CHAPTER 49

"Ah! Welcome, Doctor and Mrs. Dorsett. What a pleasant surprise. What brings you to my headquarters, may I ask?" said Commandant Zapata.

Basil said, "Since you are holding us without a valid reason and have not given a time for our release to return to the United States, we must send notifications to family, friends, and business. We don't want to arouse suspicion that we're being held on an island controlled by the Panama military without cause. It looks prejudiced since some guests had their passports returned and they left the island. We are being held against our will. Our family, friends, and business will have to act. Don't you agree, Commandant?"

Liza looked on at the impasse between Basil and Zapata in amusement. *What balls! No wonder this man makes my heart beat faster and my loins yearn for his touch.*

"Hmm. I see your point, Doctor. We don't want our methods misunderstood, creating an international incident or inspire propaganda. I will have your passports back to you by the morning, if that is okay?" Zapata said.

"That will be fine, Commandant. Thank you."

"Now, let's see what you can tell me about the mind of a killer or killers. We still don't know if there is one or two. We have three victims. Do you think there is only one killer for all three murders, Doctor, or do you think there is more than one?"

"You mentioned notes, a book of sorts, with both Agent Bradshaw and the person poisoned, Señor...."

"Alejandro Otoya," Zapata interjects.

"Yes, yes. May I look at those notes?" Basil asked.

Zapata calls out to the officer on duty to get the note books from the safe.

"Here you are, Doctor. The Diplomatic Security Service and the Department of State have read through these note books. They came up with nothing. They could not interpret them either from the poor writing or the codes. Something spilled on some of the writing and they were *manchado*," Zapata explained.

"You mean smeared? The ink is smeared?" Liza asked.

"Yes, Mrs. Dorsett. Forgive me. Some words just come naturally in my Spanish. Yes, some of the pages have smears."

"Can I take them with me?" Basil asked. "I will return them tomorrow when we pick up our passports."

" Mrs. Dorsett, you have a prudent man here. I will trust you as you have trusted me to return your passports. I release them to you," Zapata said, giving instructions to his officer to prepare release forms for Basil's signature,

"As you once said, Commandant, I did not fall off the turnip truck either."

Zapata burst into hearty laughter. "How do you say... touché?

Basil and Liza rushed out of Zapata's H.Q. faster than bees chasing their hives' attacker.

"Basil, do you think you can decode their notes? Zapata said the Diplomatic Security Service and the Department of State's office read through these note books, and they couldn't decipher them."

"My Liza, don't worry your gorgeous self. I will give it my all. I want you to help me. We need to go back to the hotel, have lunch, sit, and relax then look at all this."

"Me? You think I can help? I don't know... Are you sure Basil?"

CHAPTER 50

Basil set the dishes to the side of the table before opening each book with care.

"Careful, Basil. If you spill your drink on the pages, Zapata will crucify us."

"They're already smeared. I can't see what it says. Look at this. There are a lot of smudges."

He handed an open page to Liza. "What do you see?"

"I see a bunch of gibberish."

"Look again, don't let your eyes deceive you. The mind can play tricks on the eyes. Just like the expressions, 'Beauty is in the eye of the beholder,' or 'Your eyes are bigger than your stomach.'"

Liza stared at the pages. "Maybe I need another drink." She held her hand up for the waiter to see.

"I guess another *could* open your mind's eye," Basil suggested.

"I want to get through with this so we can get our passports and get off this island. I will never come back."

The waiter brought another round of vodka martinis.

"Now that is refreshing," Liza said, sipping, sliding the olive off the toothpick into her mouth. "Just the way I like them."

"I like how you work that olive into your mouth," Basil said.

"Something I learned a long time-ago." Liza's enigmatic smile disclosed nothing.

"Now, look again. Tell me what you see." Basil asked.

"Well, I see the jumbled alphabet, not in any order. Looks like a bunch of mish-mash to me," Liza answered, taking another sip of her martini. "Who wrote these notes?"

"Good, very good," Basil praised. "These are from the poisoned man at the café."

"Good?" Liza questioned. "What's so great about not being able to read jumbled letters?"

"Believe me, it is good that you see that. Now, look at this page of notes." He handed Liza the second book from Agent Bradshaw.

"This is different. It has jumbled letters like the first book, but it also has dots. A lot of dots going in all directions mixed with the letters. How do you make sense of all this? Again, if the Panamanian Diplomatic Security Service read through these notebooks, and they couldn't decipher them, how are we... you, going to figure it out?" questioned Liza.

"Maybe they did just fall off the turnip truck. I have to agree with you. The Diplomatic Security Service should have deciphered these codes with no problem."

"Basil, are you telling me, you know what these say... that quick?" Liza asked.

"Yes!"

"How? How the hell were you able to discover what this gibberish says? Are you going to tell me you're some secret agent man hiding behind the cloak of a psychiatrist? Maybe you should have worked for the United States Secret Service or The Agenzia Informazioni e Sicurezza Esterna.[11]

"No. Look, listen, and learn. This is so simple; they missed it. They are looking for some sophisticated code when it is the simplest."

---

[11] Italian: External Intelligence and Security Agency), commonly known as AISE is the foreign intelligence service of Italy.

"Now you just said codes, plural. Over one code?" Liza asked.

"Yes. Let me show you." Basil sketched a diagram on a napkin. "Look. The first one, as you say, is gibberish with all the letters jumbled. I know it as the Caesar Cipher."

"What is Caesar Cipher?"

"This," Basil said as he continued to draw on the napkin, "is a code Julius Caesar invented when he sent letters. He invented it so if an enemy robbed his messenger of that letter, the robber wouldn't be able to read it. It is one of the simplest codes ever. He substituted each letter by the letter that was 3 places further along in the alphabet, so that A would be D, B would be E, and C would be F, D would be G, and so on, and so on."

A B C D E F G H I J K L M N O P Q R S T U V W X Y Z

D E F G H I J K L M N O P Q R S T U V W X Y Z A B C

"Huh? Let me see that. Holy shit! I can figure out what he said as long as I have your drawing. This is crazy," Liza blurted.

"Okay, tell me. What does this say?" Basil asked.

"Meeting at café tomorrow. Pick up cash."

"Perfect. Now this? He pointed to another note.

"Locker number xiz. That I don't get," Liza said.

"You're doing good, Liza. He is also using the letters to equal numbers for the locker. X is 1 and I is 12 and Z is 3. So, he is saying XIZ is locker number 1123. Zapata had to try every locker until the key fit. It must have taken hours. Now look at this book from Agent Bradshaw again."

"Again, mixed dots in all directions and jumbled letters. Do you know what the dots mean?" Liza asked.

"Yes, I do."

My God! He's amazing. How can I be sure he'll share the money in the bank, and he's not plotting to leave me out? The thought shot unbidden through her mind.

"I learned this at University. The dots are for the blind. It is Braille named after its creator, Louis Braille, a Frenchman who lost his sight when he was fifteen in a childhood accident, back in 1824. Let me draw it out. It will take a few minutes. Order another round," Basil said.

"Here, look at this," he instructed.

a	b	c	d	e	f	g	h	i	j

k	l	m	n	o	p	q	r	s	t

u	v	w	x	y	z

"Oh. Now I see why the dots are all over the place," Liza said. "Let me see if I can tell what Agent Bradshaw wrote. Wait! There are also the jumbled letters mixed with the dots."

"You can do it. Take your time, combine the dots to line up to the matching letters, and use Caesar's Cipher code to line up the letters. Then you can combine them and spell it out." Basil suggested. "Look at the part that is legible."

"Meet bar tender before five," Liza said.

"Excellent. Not too difficult once you know how to decode it, no?"

"I get what you're saying. So, Agent Bradshaw planned to meet Felix, the bartender, before five. He murdered Felix," Liza summed up.

"Although your decoding skills are very good and you are a fast learner, do not cast your vote so fast." Basil praised Liza for her quick understanding of Bradshaw's more complex notes, combining two different codes instead of the simpler one of the poisoned man at the cafe.

"However, Zapata cannot incriminate him on circumstantial evidence. It seems Agent Bradshaw was with or planned to meet someone—we assume it was Felix—before the murderer killed him. But keep in mind your theory won't hold up."

"Why?" Liza asked.

"Agent Bradshaw died before Felix, remember?"

"Okay, then you can show Zapata and let him determine where Agent Bradshaw fits into this mess, and who killed Felix, and who poisoned the guy at the café. Maybe these codes will end this investigation. Maybe with what the murdered man at the café said about meeting someone, Zapata can put two and two together. He's the detective, not you. Although you could have been," Liza said feeling the effects of the vodka. "There's a lot here for you to go through. You finish it; I'll order another drink."

I hope he doesn't find out what I did when I was younger and try to cheat me out of all that stash.

Basil worked diligently decoding all the scribbling he could read. It was difficult to decipher through the smeared ink. After he'd spent considerable time, he did not find names, just times and locations to meet or find things, like the locker at the airport and the cash Bradshaw got from another shakedown, now in his box at the bank.

"Now what, now that you're done?" asked Liza, a slight buzz humming in her head.

"Now," stated Basil, "it's show time…"

"What's done cannot be undone" -Shakespeare

CHAPTER 51

Another night of drinking and a last show with Rachel Kazz had its effect as the morning sunlight peeked through the curtains. Basil's words were always perfect. He knew what to say and when to say them, unlike Calvin or other men Liza'd known. This time was no different. He passed from her lips, to her neck, to her breasts, to her inner thighs, describing her beauty at each touch. Liza listened to Basil's accented baritone, felt his breath roll over her like the bliss of a hot steam bath she loved so much. No matter how hungover they were in the morning, they always made love, and make love they did–twice!

"Liza, let's grab a shower and some coffee. We'll go to the Commandant's office and present our quid pro quo."

"What are you talking about?"

"These notebooks for our passports. This for that."

"Are you going to tell him how you deciphered them?"

"I think I will tell him I determined the Caesar Cipher. It is common, but it is not usual to combine it with Braille. Even that man poisoned at the cafe, Alejandro Otoya, knew the Caesar Cipher. He must have served in the army of his country. Agent Bradshaw trained with the U.S. Marshals. The military routinely teach the code to officers.

I wonder if Calvin knew it?

CHAPTER 52

"Please have a seat. I'll let Commandant Zapata know you are here," said the officer on duty.

"Show them in at once," Zapata ordered.

"Good morning, Doctor, Mrs. Dorsett," said Zapata in a robust greeting. "I hope you have good news for me, Doctor."

"Yes and no, Commandant."

"I'm listening. You say, 'yes and no?' Please explain."

"There are two different codes in the notebooks."

"Yes, yes, we know that," Zapata snapped with impatience. "Proceed."

Liza wore her tantalizing summer dress, the one that Montebello's roving eye appreciated. She leaned forward, resting her arms on Zapata's desk to distract him. She seemed to do what she intended.

"Let's look at the first one, the one with the English alphabet. It is one of the oldest codes known to man. It's called—"

"Caesar's Cipher," Zapata finished with a thinly veiled, smug smile, although fixated on Liza's braless display. "We know that one. I thought you would know it and tell me the truth. Commendable, Doctor, but we have the information from Alejandro Otoya's notebook. It is the other one, Agent Bradshaw's, we can't understand. I hoped you could do that one."

"Believe me, Commandant, Basil worked on it all day and most of the night," Liza said with a deep sigh.

"Ahem," Zapata cleared his throat. "I'm certain he did, Mrs. Dorsett. I hope he didn't desert you for too long."

Liza smiled.

"So, Commandant, as I was saying," Basil said, to get Zapata's attention.

"I'm sorry, Doctor, continue."

"The second notebook is more complex. I could not comprehend how Agent Bradshaw used both the English alphabet and dots. It made no sense to me. It must be a more sophisticated system from the United States Department of Justice and their Secret Service, do you agree?" Basil asked. *How fast did they break the code?* "And the smudges made it even more difficult to read."

"That is apparent, Doctor. When I said our own Department of State's Diplomatic Security Service could not understand it, I lied." He glanced at Basil, then at Liza, tagging their reactions.

Basil and Liza froze.

"The Department employs educated men, like yourself. We, I mean the Diplomatic Service, broke the code used by Agent Bradshaw. We got the information we needed, then we smeared the ink. We did not want to share what we found. We also wanted to see if you would tell us the truth. I thank you for your efforts, and you, Mrs. Dorsett."

Zapata was not lying. Well-schooled in the human anatomy and body language, Basil saw his pupils were not dilated, nor did he blink rapidly. He did not cross his arms, although he continued to focus on Liza. Basil had been certain the Diplomatic Security Service could not interpret

Bradshaw's notes, and yet they did. *So, the turnip truck theory is off the table. Zapata duped me. Shit!*

"You mentioned that you had to reach business, family, and friends." Zapata said, pushing the telephone toward Liza as he leaned over her. "Be my guest."

Liza knew Zapata was trying for a better view and turned to Basil for assurance.

"We won't have to use your telephone, Commandant, since you are returning our passports today."

"Oh, yes, that!" Zapata said with a frown as though considering.

CHAPTER 53

"Damn it, Basil! Zapata took us for a ride. He put us on the turnip truck. Zapata played us like a fiddle. He's not stupid. How is it you, of all people, schooled in that mind shit, could not tell he was playing us?" Liza ranted without taking a breath.

"Believe me, I used everything the University taught me and my experience. I could not put my finger on it. And you're right. He played us."

"What does he have up his sleeve? He's holding several passports, including ours. Do you think he'll trace the telephone numbers we called from his phone?" Liza asked, becoming more and more exasperated.

"What difference does it make? They are all legitimate numbers with innocent people on the other end. At least you got your messages out," Basil soothed Liza.

"What about you? Don't you have to reach anyone? Your secretary or patients?"

"No! I told you I took care of my affairs before I left the States. I don't have to answer to anyone or be anywhere."

"Well, I guess at this point in my life, I don't have to be anywhere either… with all that money we have."

Is that sarcasm? From this New York waitress? Her outrage amused Basil.

"We still have to get off this damn island and out of Panama."

"You know, Liza, you just said something very profound. Why should we worry? We can stay here, you know."

"Fuck, no! Not me! I don't think you want to stay here under suspicion either." Liza was emphatic.

"Look, we got one thing off the table, and an important one. You sent a message to everyone on your list. Now we have to think. Why are we being held? What was on the pages they smeared with ink?"

"Good question," Liza said. "but one we're not likely to know until the Commandant wants to tell us. Why don't we meet with the others whose passports he's holding? Let's compare notes; see what he told them. There's only a handful." *Zapata has a reason he's holding us. He sees something about Basil and he's holding me as leverage. But why hold the other passports?*

They proceeded to the dining room as scheduled. After being together day after day, and night after night, they knew who the guests were and where they came from. Many were from the States. Liza's first emotion on seeing the men and women gathered there was surprise; her second was gratification. Now that they were together, she wondered. *Why me? Why is Zapata holding my passport?*

They comprised the same group on the boat to Zapata's headquarters, minus the two single men. There were three couples, the mouthy, single woman, Basil and Liza.

"Good morning, everyone," Basil greeted them. "We wondered if you—"

The same woman who gave Zapata backtalk about being single and on the island to find romance interrupted him. "He plays dumb, then BAM! Now what do we do? Why am I here? I'm a single woman, you are all couples. We're the only ones whose passports he's holding. Does he think I killed these people, or is he keeping me here as a decoy, to throw you all off? I didn't kill anyone. Maybe it was one of you." She pointed to each table.

"You say!" a man from the rear table said. "How do we know you didn't do it? Or any of us?"

There was an immediate conversational buzz. Someone said, "Yours too?"

"Yes, ours too," Liza answered.

"That's a good analogy," Basil said. "Zapata, as we all know now, is not Inspector Lestrade[12]. He hoped we would get together, like we are now. He wants to pit us against each other. He threw you into the mix to stir things up," speaking to the opinionated woman, "just as you did, dismissing yourself as a suspect and pointing to the rest of us... couples who could work in concert to commit these crimes."

"What are you, a shrink?" asked the woman.

"I am educated in psychiatry," Basil said. "May I ask your name?"

"Like it matters. It's Diana, Diana Dunston. Call me DeeDee."

"Well, it matters, DeeDee. Shakespeare was right to ask what's in a name. Names matter. Words and names have a psychological effect—"

"Here comes the psychobabble bullshit," DeeDee retorted.

"Maybe to you," Basil responded. "A rose smells sweet and has such meaning. What if we called it thorny stems? Would it be as appealing? All words and names have a psychological effect."

"Well, does my name influence you, or anyone here?" DeeDee asked.

---

[12] Inspector Lestrade - a fictional character from Sherlock Holmes mysteries, had almost no skill at actual crime solving; his tenacity and determination are what brought him to the highest ranks in the official police force.

"Why do you call yourself, DeeDee? You, or someone in your youth, started calling you that and you thought it cute and catchy… maybe it attracted the boy's notice, while Diana is more suited to a woman looking for romance." Basil offered his expertise, and those around her nodded or mumbled agreement.

"Okay, lesson learned. I'll think about it. So why are we here?" she asked.

"Zapata kept you for the reason I said. Calling yourself by a nickname gives the aura of aloofness, unconcern, and smooth enough to be a killer."

"Fuck that!" DeeDee exclaimed. "I'm not a killer. What about what you said, about couples being able to help one another, maybe plan a murder? Three murders. Maybe we should put our heads together and try to understand why Zapata is holding our passports." She shrugged. "I'll start."

CHAPTER 54

Each person shared what they wanted, and after much deliberation, everyone relaxed, became more open. The liquor took over the conversations. No one gave any credence to the proverbial saying of wise King Solomon of those who drank too much: "… Wine mocks, liquor makes them noisy, and everyone under the influence is unwise. In the end it bites like a snake and stings like a viper."

Commandant Zapata's strategy was working. He assumed Basil would gather everyone to figure out what he was thinking. He hoped their drinking would loosen their minds and tongues, and someone would slip and incriminate himself.

Each guest gave their take on each of the murders and vivid accounts of how they would have done such villainous deeds. Some knew from the picture Zapata showed them that Agent Bradshaw was shot in the head. They did not know how Felix or Alejandro Otoya died until Basil informed them. At that point, the group barked accusations, raised questions, and demanded answers.

"How do you know all this?"

"Who told you?"

"Why weren't we told?"

"Maybe it was you, since you know all the details."

"Calm down everyone," Basil said. "Commandant Zapata told me. He asked me to help."

"Help how?"

"Do you know more besides what you told us?"

"Can you prescribe drugs as a psychiatrist? Maybe it was you who poisoned that man."

"Are you and your lady friend working for Zapata?" DeeDee asked.

"Let me explain. First, Zapata wants to pit each of us against the others. Listen to yourself. We must work together to determine why all of us are here, why he is holding our passports. He has ours too. He's playing poker with our lives, and he has the winning hand. From what we all shared, it could be any of us. We all travel extensively. From the stamps on our passports, he must have checked the places we've been to see if there were murders during the dates we visited."

"There would be some murders, I imagine. Murders happen all over the world, every day. Am I wrong?" DeeDee asked.

"No, you are not wrong. That's an excellent point, DeeDee, or shall I call you Diana?" Basil asked.

Liza pursed her lips. *What the hell! Is he warming up to her?* She turned to Basil with a look of censure.

"Zapata will use that as circumstantial evidence. He will try to place us in the precise time frame and place of other murders that coincide with our passport information."

"Everyone?" Diana blurted.

"So, you are saying we'll have to explain when, with whom, and where we traveled?" asked someone in their midst.

"And why! Don't forget the why. That is very important. Why did you travel? Can you imagine if, by chance, any of our passports match places and dates? He could charge a conspiracy. He will not care if he steps outside the law or harms someone in his investigation. If he convinces the Diplomatic Security Service he solved three murders and makes it stick at trial, he will earn another medal, possibly a promotion. Think about that. Here we are now, all of us. If any of our passports match up to another murder by our passport stamps, it could be disastrous." Basil said.

Everyone nodded, sober now, asking each other where and when they traveled, hoping no one matched another.

CHAPTER 55

Liza mulled over what Basil said to everyone with surface calm. Underneath, she suffered full blown confusion. *I have to get out of here. I don't like where Basil is going with this. I want that fucking money.* She concentrated on the times he was not around, his lame excuses, where he went and why. Each time, a dead person showed up... *and my missing nylon. Why would the housekeeper take one and not the pair? Maybe my nylon was used to murder poor Felix. He knows Rachel Kazz. Are they involved? She made her get-away. Oh my God! I can't go back and change things. The past is the past and now is now. Can Zapata find out from here?*

"Liza, I've been thinking..."

"Okay, start flappin' those lips, 'cause I can't think of anything except escaping! I'm listening," Liza said.

"Let's say the Commandant gives us back our passports. I believe the others will blow this place as fast as possible."

"Me too."

"No! Zapata will look at who leaves and how fast they go. You heard the others; they will leave that same day. If we stay, it will show we have nothing to hide. We can enjoy our time here for the reasons we came. We can shop, enjoy the water sports, swim, go to dinner, and enjoy the show." Basil tried to entice Liza, gave her food for thought.

"Maybe, maybe not, Basil. I'm getting anxiety hanging around, waiting for Zapata's next move, aren't you?" Liza asked.

"Yeah, but…"

"But what? There's a lot spinning in my head I have to sort out."

"Here. Have a spiro." He handed her a bottle.

"No! Every time I take one of those, you leave me." *Although, they make me feel good and my mind needs to rest awhile.*

"You're imagining things, Liza."

"Why don't we all go together and demand our passports," Liza suggested.

"Hmm, it might work. Zapata will have to target one of us. He may laugh it off or he may take our demands seriously. Do you remember what we said to him?" Basil asked.

"Just about word for word… American citizens held by the military police in a foreign country without cause and against our will is raising suspicion. How will the newspapers react?"

"Close enough. Let's see if the others are on board," Basil said.

CHAPTER 56

All nine remaining suspects gathered in the Commandant's office, clamoring with demands saying what Basil had suggested.

"Calm down, please, everyone. I will listen to you," Zapata said. "Let's do this in an orderly fashion," according to military protocol. "One at a time, please. Tell me your concerns and I will tell you mine."

Diana began. "I… you, the military police, are holding us here unnecessarily against our will. We demand you return our passports so we can go about our lives. We did not kill anyone. Look at us. We are average people who came here on vacation and now you have ruined our vacation. We spent a lot of money on this holiday, money that is boosting the economy of Contadora Island!"

"Yes, what you say is true, but what can I do? We cannot undo what has taken place by turning back the clock. We can't redo this time. Do you agree?" Zapata asked a rhetorical question. "No, it can't," he answered. "This investigation is still open. I must find who did this terrible thing, this murder of three people. Put yourselves in my shoes!"

"Yes, Commandant," Basil replied. "We understand your position, but why are you holding only our passports? You returned the passports of the other guests you questioned and they have left the island and Panama."

"Because everyone here has done more traveling than the others," Zapata answered.

"So, what does that prove?" asked Diana. "I'm demanding you return my... our passports at once or I... we will go to the American Embassy in Panama."

Zapata called out to the day officer, who scurried at his command, returning with everyone's passports. He distributed them.

"Now, is everyone happy? You got your wish, Americans. Get out of my office! Come back and visit us soon," Zapata barked, with a hearty laugh.

All nine stampeded from his office. Indistinct chatter alluded to getting the first transport plane out of Panama.

"So, Basil. Now what? We have our way out. We can take our money and go back home... to New York, where I want to be."

"I understand your growing anxiety, Liza, but Zapata will not take these passports back. He realized what we presented to him as a united group was threatening, and he had no just cause to keep us. I think our plan worked because of our innocence. If any of the nine of us was guilty, we wouldn't act so forceful. There may be a killer among us or someone on the island, even an islander. Let's not rush to judgment as to our get-a-way. Let's plan our escape. That's what it will be: an escape from injustice and prejudice."

"I don't agree. Zapata's job is to catch a killer and he's doing it. I think he has a great responsibility here. He has to do whatever it takes. Once everyone leaves, his odds diminish, and that is not good for him. He must have thought it was a guest at the hotel and not an island resident. Maybe he is right. Maybe an imported killer, a hit man."

"Wow! Liza, your imagination is hard at work. Let's go back to the hotel, grab a bite, and relieve some of our tension with a drink," Basil suggested.

CHAPTER 57

Basil's breath moved over her skin, bringing his lips to hers. Captivated by her hazel eyes, Basil froze for a moment, admiring them. He knew they held a secret somewhere in their depths. As the poets wrote, eyes are the windows to the soul, and Liza's soul hid a secret. He didn't care at that moment as he gently caressed her shoulder, gliding down the curve of her back, with a slight stroking motion. Her skin was like satin, pressed against his muscular physique she so admired. Basil's eyes lingered on her uncovered beauty as their clothes drifted from them. His lustful gaze stoked her passion making her want him even more.

Basil enjoyed the scent of her tawny skin. It was natural, fresh, inviting, and hers alone. Each interlude began in the present, extending outside of time: no past, no future, only now. No obstructions, no questions, no doubts… just what they saw in each other's eyes, or felt on their bodies with not even a sound. They made love that only a select few ever experienced. This time they felt no urgency. Face to face, lost in their artistry.

They felt a difference this time, as peace replaced their previous erotic behavior. It wasn't their culmination together as was their usual fashion; it was like a man's inherent fear of the dark, a preface of what must come…

CHAPTER 58

Liza's suspicion grew with Zapata's desire to use Basil for his expertise. *Did he know something? Was he waiting for Basil to slip up? Trying to catch him in a lie? Why is he so willing to share details of the investigation with Basil?*

Liza examined the puzzle pieces, trying to match the times Basil was absent, gauging the time frame of all three murders. Wasn't that what Zapata was doing? An experienced police officer and soldier like Zapata questioning timelines?

Am I in bed with a killer? Can I stop the love that is growing now that my dreams are at my fingertips? The money! The fucking money! Is it the answer or will Basil stand in my way? Neither one of us has said words of love in a long time...

"Liza," Basil called out.

"I'm right here, don't shout. What is it?"

"You may be right. We should plan to leave like the others. There's a new breed of tourist checking into the hotel. They will cause chaos for a spell."

"Wait 'til they find out the romance, pirates' ghosts and buried treasure described in the brochure on their wonderful island of enchantment holds an unsolved murder mystery," Liza said.

"Why the change of heart?" Basil questioned.

"Three murders and none of them solved. How is it that Zapata, with so little resistance, gave up all our passports? He has something up his sleeve. I don't believe that a man who has been to war, earned all those medals and lost an eye, who is so conniving and gaslighted everyone, is letting this go. You're the one with the psychological degree. Do you think the nine of us are going away scot-free? No, no, and no. It's too easy."

"I see your point. We better make use of our time. Why don't you pack and I'll arrange our flight out of here?" Basil suggested.

"What about all our money? We can't leave it. Who knows what will happen to it? I'm not leaving without that money, Basil," Liza was adamant.

"We can come back for it. It will be secure in the bank."

"How can you be sure? You see how the authorities are running this island and this country. If we leave without our money, Zapata may seize it. I will not let that happen," Liza was emphatic.

"All right. I'll book our tickets and we'll go to the bank," Basil said.

CHAPTER 59

Liza was right on target. Bullseye! Before Basil could pick up the phone, Zapata and his officers were back at the hotel. He stopped two of the seven others whose passports he returned as they prepared to board their flight at the airport.

The clamoring was loud and profane. They questioned their detainment for more questioning in strident voices.

"Why are we back here? You returned our passports. That meant we were clear to go. I want the American Embassy notified."

"I will go to the newspapers when I get back to the States. This is false imprisonment. I demand you get your Diplomatic Service here."

Diana, who voiced her opinion multiple times in a loud and clear voice earlier, sat quiet as a church mouse.

"Everyone will voice, once again, whatever they want. My officers will escort you to separate rooms for additional questioning. We discovered some additional information," Zapata said, unmoved by the din.

"Thank you, Diana. Outstanding job. You may go now," Zapata said.

"What the hell is going on?" Liza asked.

"Diana is an undercover officer with our pólice. She discovered important information to our investigation. We will review once again what we've already covered. So, everyone will go to separate rooms."

Liza sat alone in the first room, almost in tears. She steadied herself when Zapata entered, confident she had nothing to hide.

Zapata greeted her. "Mrs. Dorsett, it is Elizabetta Dorsett, Elizabetta Gianno correct?" He placed a file on the table in front of her.

"What is this?" Liza asked. She opened the file to uncover her mug shot and arrest records.

"You know what it is. It may have been years ago, but maybe not. Maybe you are still a prostitute. Perhaps you are taking advantage of Doctor Caprio. You know..." Zapata suggested using sex to scam him.

"This was years ago. Look at the dates. Why do you have my file?" Liza demanded. "I want an American Embassy Envoy now."

"All in due time, Mrs. Dorsett. We have three murders to solve and we must make an arrest. We brought back everyone with criminal records."

"Why are you harping on this? This was years ago. I did what I had to do." Liza said.

"Yes, Mrs. Dorsett. Many of us do things we later regret, knowing we could have chosen an alternate path, but your path led you here to me. From your past, it seems you are a femme fatale. You know. A seductive woman whose charms ensnare her lovers, often compromising a man and leading him to do illegal and deadly deeds. Maybe you killed or had these men killed," he said to intimidate her.

Liza controlled herself. *This fucker is serious. He's trying to stick me with these murders. Stay calm, think.*

"Comm-an-dant Za-pa-ta," Liza stammered. "This was me almost ten years ago, not now. I work hard as a waitress in a diner in New York City. I'm not a killer or a femme fatale."

"This file shows me different. Your record shows several arrests from 1940 to 1943 and you knew some not so nice characters."

"That was then. It's all in there," she closed the folder. "I was not part of the criminal world. Those men were clients. They were just clients. I also had police, like yourself, as clients. All the men were paying clients. It was not personal," Liza said, composed by now.

"What can you tell me about Dr. Caprio... Basil?" Zapata asked.

"What do you want to know? I'm sure you know more than I do. If you got a copy of my file from years ago, you must have one on Basil or he wouldn't be here. I'd like to know what you have and why he is here," Liza said.

"Well, Mrs. Dorsett, he had a run-in with the authorities in New York and in Italy. New York State revoked his medical license, and..."

"What! Are you fucking playing with me?" Liza blurted.

Zapata saw the shock on her face. She had not known of Basil's arrest records.

How did he get the medication he gave me? I've been sleeping with a criminal. Then she realized. *Basil was sleeping with a criminal too.*

"Now, Mrs. Dorsett, back to my question. Tell me what you know about Dr. Caprio. Were you with him every minute or were there times he wasn't around?"

Liza remembered stories of people jailed in foreign prisons who disappeared. She didn't want to be one of them, ending up in some God-forsaken country at the mercy of some unwashed, repulsive jailer. She related her time with

Basil from the time she saw him in the airport gift shop until Zapata brought them to his headquarters, leaving nothing out.

CHAPTER 60

Liza did not see Basil before Commandant Zapata escorted her back to the hotel. *What will happen to Basil? I didn't suspect he was capable of violence, that he was arrested for aggravated assault with a deadly weapon. How the hell did he get his sentence reduced? He only served two years in prison. My God! If the Commandant proves he is involved in these murders, what will happen to me?*

Liza ran to the door before the third knock and threw open the door.

"Basil, thank God you're..."

"Sorry to disappoint you, Mrs. Dorsett," Commandant Zapata said. "We have charged Dr. Caprio with murder—all three murders. The information you provided along with the mysterious disappearance of one nylon helped us determine his guilt. We *suspect* he used the nylon stocking to kill Felix. What Diana witnessed, and her information added to our timeline. Everything we discovered appears to point to Dr. Caprio."

"No..." Liza whimpered.

"We deciphered the coded notebooks and smeared them, as I showed you, before Dr. Caprio saw them. We did not want him to see what was in them. The notes from Agent Bradshaw and Alejandro Otoya mentioned Dr. Caprio by name. Agent Bradshaw's notes called him "hit man Capri.""

" No! No! It can't be," Liza cried, as tears streamed down her face. "You're making a mistake."

"I'm sorry, Mrs. Dorsett. We are here to gather his belongings. We must search through them. Where are his belongings? We must take them with us. Maybe you should gather your belongings together and arrange your departure," Zapata suggested.

"I want to see Basil," Liza demanded.

"That is not possible, Mrs. Dorsett. We have moved Dr. Caprio to our prison in Panama by the order of the Ministry of Government and Justice. It is hours away, perhaps a day's ride. You cannot communicate with him until his trial, and that may take months... perhaps one year. I believe it would be best if you return home. Where are his belongings?"

"There. Everything is right there." Liza pointed.

"I do not see the satchel I saw when we were here last," Zapata questioned.

"It must be in the bathroom with his razor and things. I will get it." Liza removed the key to the bank deposit box before giving it to Zapata.

"I am sorry, Mrs. Dorsett," Zapata said, turning and leaving with his officers. Liza collapsed in a chair, confused, numb, not knowing what to do. She was alone with no one to call or offer comfort. She lapsed into a daze. *I wish I had a spiro. What the fuck should I to do? What am I going to do? Basil, you son of a bitch. I could kill you! Why? God damn it! I was in love with you.*

CHAPTER 61

Devastated, Liza left her room to purchase vodka. Two days passed before she came to her senses. She knew she had to move on, but she was unemployed and aimless. This time, however, she would not have to prostitute herself. She realized she was rich beyond her imagination. *My God, this happened so I can fulfill the dream I had with Calvin. I deserve this.* Gathering herself, Liza packed her belongings and booked her flights, but she would go to Panama City National Bank before her departure.

Liza wore Montebello's favorite summer dress with the thin spaghetti straps allowing the neckline to sit low on her breasts when she sauntered into the lobby of the bank. Her past taught her how to use her assets, and she flaunted them.

"Ah, Señora Caprio, what a pleasure to see you. And where is the doctor?" Señor Montebello asked.

"He's not feeling well. He sent me to get something from the safe deposit box, if you please." Liza smiled and fluttered her long lashes at him.

"Why, yes, Señora. Come, let us go," Montebello obliged, leading her to the vault.

She handed him the key to the box, and Montebello inserted his key. He removed the box for her and placed it on the table. Montebello, as usual, lingered, feasting his eyes on her breasts.

"Señor Montebello, you're a married man," she reminded him, prodding his frozen gaze and jolting him to reality. Liza knew that slight embarrassment would be awkward for a man in his position. He would not question her further about Basil. She filled her valise with the bank book and the cash — all of it. Calling Montebello back to replace the box, he returned her key, although she wouldn't need it.

"Señora, my humble apologies. I meant no disrespect..."

"I forgive you," Liza interrupted, walking out with her head high. She did not give him the usual one-hundred-dollar bill.

CHAPTER 62

Liza's plane landed at Idlewild Airport, an everyday occurrence. Departing passengers hurried to their gates or arrivals struggled with baggage to the cabs outside the terminal. Walking into the gift shop where she first saw Basil, the love she still felt for him brought memories to mind. Happy to be back in New York, she froze at the banner headline on the front page of her favorite newspaper. She reached for a copy, dropping several coins on the cashier's counter.

**RACHEL KAZZ, SINGING SENSATION,
AT MOBSTER PAUL CASERTA'S FUNERAL**

She studied the picture, a blurry long-distance shot of a woman in dark clothes, then read the caption.

MISS KAZZ, FORMALLY SYLVIA CASERTA, SHOWN ARRIVING AT WOODLAWN CEMETERY TO ATTEND THE FUNERAL OF HER FATHER, TWO-TON PAULIE CASERTA.

STORY PAGE SIX, GRACE TILLY

I would like to thank you for choosing my novels. Certainly, this is an important part of my journey as an author.

One of the ways to enrich readership is with reviews. Amazon, Barnes & Noble, I-books, Kindle, Nook as all online booksellers, use reviews in their algorithms for book placement.

Please place a review on Amazon.com for me.

Thank you and I look forward to seeing you in my next novel.

fred berri

References
The *American Church* in Paris, located at Quai d'Orsay, Paris, France, is the first American church established outside the United States tracing its roots back to 1814. The American Church in Paris is an inter-denominational fellowship for all those adhering to the historic Christian tradition as expressed in the Apostles' Creed. Its architecture is magnificent Gothic Revival.

Songs:
"It Had To Be You."
Composer- Isham Jones
Published- Jerome H. Remic & Co.

"The One I Love Belongs to Somebody Else."
Music- Isham Jones
Lyrics- Gus Kahn
Published 1924

Billie Holiday: Born Eleanora Fagan 1915
Billy Holiday had a seminal influence on jazz music and pop singing. Her vocal style, strongly inspired by jazz instrumentalists, pioneered a new way of manipulating phrasing tempo. She was known for her vocal delivery and improvisational skills.

Ava Gardner: Born Ava Lavinia Gardner 1922
Ava Gardner was an American actress and singer under contract with Metro-Goldwyn-Mayer.

Cover: Google Images

CPSIA information can be obtained
at www.ICGtesting.com
Printed in the USA
LVHW111157170520
655737LV00003B/229